Without your shining encouragement, laughter and love,
this book wouldn't exist. This is for you, Grania.

—M. Y.

SIMON SPOTLIGHT
An imprint of Simon & Schuster Children's Publishing Division
1230 Avenue of the Americas, New York, New York 10020
This Simon Spotlight hardcover edition September 2019
© 2019 Mark Young and The Jim Henson Company
JIM HENSON'S mark & logo, FRANKEN-SCI HIGH mark & logo, characters, and elements are trademarks of The Jim Henson Company. All Rights Reserved.
All rights reserved, including the right of reproduction in whole or in part in any form.
SIMON SPOTLIGHT and colophon are registered trademarks of Simon & Schuster, Inc.
For information about special discounts for bulk purchases, please contact Simon & Schuster Special Sales at 1-866-506-1949 or business@simonandschuster.com.
Manufactured in the United States of America 0819 FFG
10 9 8 7 6 5 4 3 2 1
ISBN 978-1-4814-9134-1 (hc)
ISBN 978-1-4814-9133-4 (pbk)
ISBN 978-1-4814-9135-8 (eBook)

MONSTERS AMONG US!

Summit Free Public Library

CREATED BY **MARK YOUNG**
TEXT WRITTEN BY **TRACEY WEST**
ILLUSTRATED BY **MARIANO EPELBAUM**

Simon Spotlight
New York London Toronto Sydney New Delhi

CHAPTER 1

Pass the Portal!

"Ca-wee! Ca-wee! Ca-wee!"

Newton Warp opened his eyes. In front of him, a purple fuzzy monster with a snout like a trumpet was hovering in the air, flapping its wings.

"Ca-wee! Ca-wee! Ca-wee!" The shrill, annoying sound streamed out of the monster's snout.

"All right, all right, I'm awake," Newton mumbled.

He threw off his covers and jumped down off the top bunk. The monster followed him, still making noise.

He ducked his head into his roommate's bottom bunk.

"Higgy! There's a flying monster in here! Is this supposed to be happening?" he asked.

The blob of green goo under the covers stirred, and two eyeballs peeked out.

"A monster? I would guess that your friend Shelly has something to do with that," Higgy replied. "Now,

if you'll excuse me, I'm not awake yet." He rolled over.

Shelly, of course! Newton realized. He picked up the tablet on top of his dresser and tapped on Shelly's name.

A tiny hologram of Shelly's face appeared in front of him. She grinned.

"Oh good! Woller found you," Shelly said.

"Woller? You mean that's its name?" Newton asked, brushing the monster away from his face.

"He's my latest creation. He's one part butler and one part annoying alarm clock," Shelly said. "I sent him to wake you up. We've got that early morning meeting with Headmistress Mumtaz, remember?"

"How could I forget?" Newton asked. "You know how important this is to me."

"Well, hurry up and get ready," Shelly said. "We don't want to be late."

"Ca-wee! Ca-wee!"

"And what do I do with Woller?" Newton asked.

"Just let him follow you," Shelly said, and then her face disappeared.

Newton sighed, grabbed a towel and a small bag, and headed to the bathroom down the hall in the dormitory. Still half asleep, he stopped in front of the mirror and yawned. Then he tasted peppermint.

Woller had stuck a toothbrush in Newton's mouth and

was brushing Newton's teeth. When Newton stepped
toward the sink to rinse out his mouth, Woller beat
him to it and gave him a cup filled with water. Newton
shrugged and decided to let the monster take care of
him. It was almost like being asleep while someone
else took care of the boring stuff. Woller turned on the
shower and when the temperature was perfect, nudged
Newton in. Then the shower's usual features took over.
The walls were outfitted with lights that changed color

according to the mood of the person showering. They quickly switched from a neutral silver to a peaceful, glowing blue, and relaxing music started to play. As two robot arms scrubbed Newton's hair, Newton started to feel more awake. The color of the shower turned to a cheerful yellow, and the music became more upbeat. When Newton started singing along, a robotic arm sprang out of the wall and shoved a waterproof karaoke microphone at him! Newton didn't really know the words, of course, so he suddenly got a little sad.

So much had happened since that day, just a few weeks ago, that he'd woken up in Franken-Sci High. He had no memory—just a student ID card and a strange bar code on his foot. Luckily, he'd met Shelly Ravenholt and her friend Theremin Rozika, and they helped him get used to the strange school for mad scientists, although it had been a rocky start.

As a robot arm scrubbed his back, Newton thought back to his first days at Franken-Sci High. Theremin was an underachieving robotic student with an anger management problem. He'd been best friends with Shelly before Newton showed up on campus and had quickly become jealous of Newton and Shelly's fast friendship. Thanks to Headmistress Mumtaz's intervention, they'd worked things out. Then Shelly, Theremin, and Newton had worked on a project for

the Mad Science Fair—and won! The prize was a special portal pass that Newton hoped would help him find out who he really was and where he came from.

He turned off the water and wrapped himself in a towel, stopping to scratch the bar code on his foot. Then he went back to his dorm room and got dressed. Soon he was outside, heading from the dorm to the main school building. Woller flew by his shoulder, now making a happier sound.

"Too-doo! Too-doo!"

A colorful bird flew down from a palm tree and stared at Woller for a moment before flying away. The outside air was warm and muggy—the school was somewhere on an island in the middle of the Bermuda Triangle. Shelly had explained that it was a region in the Atlantic Ocean where mysterious things happened—like ships that vanished into thin air while sailing through its waters. With its phosphorescent electrical fog that made it impossible to locate, the Bermuda Triangle was the perfect hiding place for a school for mad scientists.

As he approached the front doors of the main building, they opened automatically with a *swoosh*. He stepped along the yellow-and-green linoleum floor to the locker banks and stopped in front of his locker, number 352.17.

He quickly began the three-step process to unlock it.

First, he pressed his finger to the button on the glass panel. *Beep!*

Next, he opened his eyes wide for the eye scan. *Beep!*

Last but not least, he licked the taste-sensitive security lines for the saliva analysis . . . and made a face at the disgusting flavor-of-the-day.

"Slug slime," Shelly said, suddenly standing next to him. "Professor Phlegm must have woken up in a bad mood this morning."

The professor was in charge of choosing the locker flavors, and if they were any indication, he seemed to be in a bad mood pretty regularly.

"Is it slug slime?" Newton asked. *Beep!* Success! Newton opened the door very, very slowly to make sure there weren't any black holes lurking inside like the time his friend Theremin almost got lost in one. The coast was clear, so Newton took out a duffel bag full of books and turned to Shelly.

"It's not *so* bad," Newton said, smacking his lips.

"Too-doo!" Woller whistled happily and flew to Shelly, landing on her shoulder.

"Thank goodness," Newton said. "He's cute, but, um, kind of irritating."

Shelly gave Woller a little pat on the head. "Aw,

you're just saying that because he woke you up," she said. "He's really very sweet."

They walked down the hall together and stopped in front of the office of Ms. Mumtaz, the school's headmistress. Theremin was waiting for them by the front door, his robotic legs hovering a few inches above the floor like they always did. The two round eyes in his metal head lit up when he saw his friends approaching.

"Are you guys ready?" Theremin asked. "This is kind of exciting. I've never won anything before."

"I'm excited too, but I'm not ready," Shelly said. "I can't decide where I want to go."

"Well, I know exactly where I want to go," Newton said cheerfully.

Theremin tapped on the door with his metal hand.

"Come in!" a voice called from inside.

They obeyed and walked into the office of the headmistress. She sat behind the desk, a birdlike woman with orange-and-purple streaked hair. They sat in chairs in front of her.

"Theremin. Shelly. Newton. Congratulations on winning first prize in Franken-Sci High's Mad Science Fair," she said. "Your wall-climbing Sticky Savers proved to be a valuable safety tool in a dangerous situation. Your invention may save lives one day." They had invented

the grippy gloves and socks after discovering that Newton's hands were strangely sticky. When they took a closer look using Theremin's retractable microscope, there were tiny hairlike structures that helped Newton cling to walls like a gecko or other reptile.

"Thanks. We're really proud of it," Shelly said, as Woller settled on her shoulder and immediately started to snore.

"*Zzzzzzzz.*"

"Now then, let's get down to business," Mumtaz said. "You have each won a special portal pass that will allow you to leave the school and travel anywhere you wish, pending your parents' approval, of course."

She held up a brochure about Franken-Sci High that was given to new students. It was made from a shimmering, ultra-thin metallic alloy. When a student folded the brochure in a specific way, it opened a portal that connected the school to the outside world. The school had specifically set up the portal system that way to keep the inventions and monstrous creatures inside the school from being stolen by the outside world— and to keep the outside world safe from the inventions created at Franken-Sci High.

"Tell me," Ms. Mumtaz continued, "have you decided where you want to go?"

"I haven't exactly decided yet," Shelly admitted. "I mean, I have lots of ideas, but it's so hard to choose! I'd love to go to the Pacific Northwest and gather hair samples of pygmy sasquatches, or maybe study the mythical flying snakes of Borneo . . ."

"Yes, well, you must decide soon," the headmistress interrupted her. "What about you, Theremin?"

"Well, I've never been anywhere before," the robot admitted. "So, I thought I'd go somewhere snowy. It never snows on the island."

"Except in World Weather Domination class," Shelly reminded him.

"Yeah, but that's no fun," Theremin said. "I want to try snowboarding. Or maybe tubing. It looks like fun."

"Um, can you remind me of what snow is?" Newton asked, feeling a little awkward. Some things he just seemed to know. But sometimes his mind was a blank.

"Frozen water crystals that fall from the sky," Theremin replied. "But when millions and millions of them fall, you can do fun stuff with them. I hear it's like fluffy white sand."

Ms. Mumtaz turned to Newton. "And what about you, Newton? Where would our newest student like to go?"

"Well . . . ," Newton began.

I want to find my family. That's what he was

thinking. But for some reason, he didn't say it out loud. Shelly looked at him curiously.

Ms. Mumtaz sighed. "Okay, then. Well, you still have some time to decide. Now let's get your parents' permission."

She took three devices from a desk drawer. She put one on a small platform on her desk and pressed a button. A green light flashed under it.

Poof! The device disappeared.

"That went to your parents, Shelly," she explained. "And here's one for your father, Theremin."

Poof!

She picked up the third device, smiled at Newton, then stopped. Since she knew that Newton had no memories of his family, there was no one he could ask to give permission.

Newton was thinking the same thing, and seeing her reach for the device and hesitate made his stomach drop with a sudden sadness. "If I don't have a family member to give me permission, does that mean I can't use my portal pass?"

The headmistress laughed. "Not to worry, *I'll* give permission! I don't mind breaking the rules now and then. Besides, I'm basically your guardian anyway."

She picked up the device intended for Newton's

family and tapped the screen. A series of audio prompts asked if she would allow Newton to use a portal pass. To give her approval, she had to complete a series of biometric tests—from a face scan to vocal cord vibrations observed when she yodeled—to confirm her identity. When the tests were complete, she gave verbal, written, and subconscious brainwave approval. The device glowed green.

"Done!" she said. Then she looked at the three of

them. "So, here are the rules. One, you can only use your portal pass on a weekend. Two, you must keep up with all homework assignments."

Theremin groaned. "That's no fun!"

"And three, you have to have a virtual chaperone go with you—a hologram of one of your professors, or another staff member from school."

Theremin groaned again. "That's even worse!"

Then the teleportation platform beeped, and one of the permission devices reappeared. Ms. Mumtaz picked it up.

"Shelly, your parents gave you permission," she reported. "They wrote, 'Of course Shelly can go! Smiley face.'"

Beep! The second permission device appeared on the teleporter. Ms. Mumtaz didn't need to read that one. It pulsed with a big red light instead of a green one and flashed a message that read, "Permission denied."

"What?" Theremin wailed. "Did Father give a reason?"

"I'm afraid not," Ms. Mumtaz replied, checking the device. "But don't worry. I'll find Professor Rozika in the lab and have a talk with him. Now, Newton, are you sure you don't have any idea where you want to go?"

"Well, I—" Newton began, but the headmistress's eyeglass lenses began to flicker. Then they transformed into translucent screens. A message scrolled across them.

"Oh dear," she said. "It looks like Professor Yuptuka

is having a hitch with her teleportation class again."

"Where did they end up this time?" Shelly asked.

"Well, apparently she was hoping for a pleasant jaunt into space," Ms. Mumtaz replied, reading. "Not allowed, of course. But now she and her class are stranded on the dark side of the moon, and while they have plenty of snack foods, their oxygen supply is running low."

The headmistress stood up. "We'll have to finish this conversation later," she said. "I've got to get our Astrophysics Department on this."

She rushed out of the office, and they followed her. Theremin kicked a metal trashcan in the hallway.

"Father ruins everything!" he complained.

"Maybe we can all go talk to him?" Newton asked.

Theremin's father taught Quantum Robotics at Franken-Sci High.

"Don't bother," Theremin replied. "He's the worst dad ever."

"Oh, Theremin," Shelly said sympathetically. "I'm sorry, but I'm sure Ms. Mumtaz will convince him eventually. Come on, let's get some breakfast."

Shelly and Theremin walked down the hall, toward the glass transport tube that led to the cafeteria. Newton hung back behind them, thinking. Theremin's dad sounded mean. What if he had a mean dad too? Would that be worse than not having a dad at all? He looked down at his green-lit permission device and sighed.

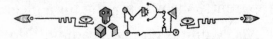

When the weekend came, Newton's plan was to ask the portal to take him home to meet his parents. He would finally learn the truth. For better or worse.

As he pondered this, he felt a prickly sensation on the back of his neck. He stopped and turned around.

Out of the corner of his eye, he saw a shape quickly dart toward him. He couldn't tell if it was human or some kind of monster. Newton's instincts kicked in and he flattened himself against a wall, and in a flash his skin and clothes changed color to match the wall perfectly. He had camouflaged himself just in time to see the figure search the hallway—looking right in his direction—before ducking into a classroom.

Newton tried to convince himself that nothing was wrong. *It must be Higgy*, he thought. *Yeah, he's working on a new prank*. His roommate was always trying to scare him in some way.

Newton turned around and ran to catch up with Theremin and Shelly, trying to put the incident out of his mind.

But why were the hairs on the back of his neck still standing on end?

Attack of the Killer Butterfly

Whoosh!

The glass tube leading to the cafeteria whisked Newton, Shelly, and Theremin to the fourth floor in seconds. Newton still hadn't gotten used to the sensation.

"Hold up a sec. I'm dizzy," Newton said as his friends hurried toward the food line.

"Sure," Theremin replied. "I guess that's one good thing about being a robot. I never get dizzy."

The smell of hot food made Newton's stomach rumble as they got in the line of kids waiting for food. After a minute he felt someone tap his shoulder, and he turned around.

"Great job at the Mad Science Fair on Saturday." It was Tori Twitcher, a freshman at the school. "I thought my robotic shark was cool, but your Sticky Savers were much more useful."

"Thanks," Newton said. He motioned to Shelly and

15

Theremin. "We all worked on it together."

Gustav Goddard walked up next to Tori. "Yeah, everyone is still laughing! When Mimi's volcano began to erupt, and she grabbed your sticky socks and gloves to climb up the walls to save herself—I've never seen her move so fast! She was so scared!"

"Ahem!"

Newton turned behind him to see Mimi Crowninshield standing there. Her arms were folded across her chest, and she was tapping her foot on the ground.

"Uh, hi, Mimi," he said.

Mimi ignored him and glared at Gustav. "I can tell you for a fact that I was *not* scared," she insisted. "If you must know, I was doing Newton a favor. Nobody was paying attention to his stupid invention until I demonstrated it. Then the judges saw that the Sticky Savers could actually be useful in emergencies."

Theremin's eyes angrily flashed red. "Oh yeah? Well—" He stopped short. Theremin was working on having better control over his emotions. "You know, you might have a point."

"Of course I do!" Mimi said smugly as she thrust her nose in the air. Then she cut in line right in front of Shelly.

Theremin nudged Shelly. "Hey, are you going to let her get away with that?"

Shelly shrugged. "It's not a big deal. Anyway, she's right. We wouldn't have won first place if Mimi's volcano hadn't erupted."

Newton nodded. Ms. Mumtaz had just awarded their Sticky Savers third prize when Mimi's volcano had started to erupt accidentally. Mimi grabbed the Sticky Savers and used them to scamper up the wall all the way to the ceiling! When the judges saw that, they awarded Newton, Shelly, and Theremin first prize.

And Shelly was right—letting Mimi cut wasn't a big deal, because the line moved quickly. Soon the three friends were sitting at their usual table, each with a plate containing one Extreme Pancake.

"Remind me why these are extreme?" Newton asked as he stared down at his pancake.

"I dunno," Theremin replied. "I don't eat, remember? I took one so I wouldn't feel left out."

"Each one contains a thousand percent of a day's nutrients and all the most popular breakfast ingredients—eggs, bacon, cereal, sausage, oatmeal, toast, and orange juice," Shelly replied. "Taste it."

Newton picked up his fork, when he heard a squishy sound behind him.

"Mind if I sit down?"

It was Higgy, dressed up for a typical day of

school in his usual gear—a bandage-covered face, dark goggles, a heavy coat, black boots, and a wool cap on his head.

"Sure," Newton said quickly, and Shelly screwed up her face.

"Sorry, Shelly, but my regular table has been taken over by Fern Faraday and her pesky two-dimensional hamsters," Higgy said, motioning. "I promise to keep my slurping to a minimum."

"Thanks," Shelly said, with a look of relief.

Higgy plopped down his plate and slid into his seat beside Shelly. A green goo tendril slithered from his coat, picked up the pancakes, and shoved it in the gap between his face bandages.

Slurp . . . slurp . . . slurp . . . strange squishy noises emerged from Higgy's face. Newton was getting used to it and could tell Higgy was trying to be quiet, or at least as quiet as possible for a kid made of goo.

Shelly pushed her plate forward.

"Not hungry today, I guess." She smiled, trying not to hurt Higgy's feelings.

"Too bad. This is delicious!" Higgy said. Then he let out a loud burp.

"By the way, Higgy, nice try earlier, trying to scare me," Newton said. "But it didn't work."

"I don't . . . *burp* . . . know what you . . . *burp* . . . mean," Higgy replied.

"Trying to sneak up on me in the hallway," Newton said.

"I swear, roomie, it wasn't . . . *burp* . . . me," Higgy protested.

"Really?" Newton said as he touched the hairs on the back of his neck. "That's weird."

"Not as weird as what happened to you at the Mad Science Fair, with those Predictive Virtual Reality Goggles," Shelly said. "You put them on, and then you started freaking out and screaming."

Another shivery feeling crept up Newton's spine as the memory returned. The goggles were another entry at the Mad Science Fair. They could show what happened to something in the past or predict what might happen to it in the future.

"It . . . it was really disturbing," Newton began. "I put on the goggles and looked at a lizard. That's when I saw the lizard growing backward in time, becoming a tadpole, and then an egg."

"Cool!" Higgy burped.

Newton nodded. "And seeing that lizard egg triggered a memory, I think. I remembered being inside a kind of a bubble or a glass pod filled with water. Then a bright

light flicked on, and I could see the shadows of people coming closer and closer. Then the glass pod started to crack . . . and then . . ."

His three friends leaned in closer.

"Then what, Newton?" Shelly gasped.

"The memory stopped. I screamed because I wanted to see what happened next."

"Sounds like the goggles malfunctioned." Theremin chuckled. "Besides, how could that have been a memory?"

"I guess you're right, but it sure felt like one," Newton said as he took a bite of his pancake.

Shelly was nodding thoughtfully. "It *is* a memory, Newton," she said. "It matches what we already know about you. You've got extra-grippy fingers and toes. You can camouflage yourself in dangerous situations. You can see in the dark, and I saw you sprout gills when you jumped into the pool."

"What does that have to do with me being in a . . . a glass pod?" Newton asked.

"I'm not sure yet," Shelly admitted. "But we do know that you're an extraspecial human. So, you must come from some extraspecial place."

"Right," Theremin laughed. "Like an extraspecial glass pod."

"I don't know," Newton said. "The pod didn't feel

special, exactly. It felt . . . strange. I just want to be like everyone else."

Higgy snorted. "Roomie, I'm made of gaseous green goo without a skeleton. So, if anyone here is not like everyone else, it's me—not you."

Shelly frowned thoughtfully. "Even so, maybe it's best if we all keep this a secret for now," she said. "Until we know more, at least."

Newton nodded. "That's fine with me. I feel like I'm just starting to fit in here. I don't want that to change."

Suddenly, the cafeteria walls changed color to a pulsing bright blue as a robotic voice calmly announced, "Period four. Time for period four."

Shelly stood up. "We'd better get to class!"

After a few weeks at the school, Newton had finally settled into a routine. Today was a Monday, so that meant he had History of Mad Scientists, followed by Neo-Evolutionary Biology, Electro-Fluid Physics, Lunch, Genetic Friendgineering, and Dark Matter Matters.

Hours later, Newton and Shelly walked out of their last class together.

"There's a meeting of the Monster Club right now," Shelly said. "Wanna come?"

"Sure," Newton replied. "I've been thinking of joining, you know, since I'm sorta not human.

Maybe I can learn something."

"Awesome!" Shelly replied. "We've been playing around with some pretty advanced stuff lately, but I'm sure you'll catch on."

"Well, you said you're related to that famous scientist, Dr. Frankenstein, right?" Newton asked. "There's a whole chapter on him in my *History of Mad Scientists* book."

Shelly nodded.

"So, do you think that's why you're good at making monsters?" Newton asked.

"Maybe," Shelly replied. "I mean, I guess it makes sense."

"And is your whole family good at it?" Newton asked. "Like, does your family get together with other Frankensteins and make monsters together and stuff?"

Shelly shook her head. "I'm a Ravenholt. We Ravenholts are all good at making monsters, but we don't hang out with the Frankensteins."

"Shelly! Newton!"

Newton felt a powerful hand slap him on the back. He caught his balance then turned to see Tootie Van der Flootin grinning at him. As usual, she had her hair tied in a braided bun on top of her head.

"You guys totally rocked the Mad Science Fair," she said.

"Thanks," Newton and Shelly said.

Tootie pushed past them into the classroom where Professor Gertrude Leviathan led the Monster Club. The professor sat at her desk, a mass of pink curls framing her face. She was wearing her trademark leopard-print lab coat and entertaining a small group of students, who seemed to hang on her every word.

"And then I said, 'If you want that horsefly to play the piano, I'm going to have to give it at least ten fingers!'" and everyone laughed. She looked up when Newton, Shelly, and Tootie entered.

"Looks like the gang's all here!" Professor Leviathan said. "Great! We can get started."

"Professor Leviathan, can I ask a question first?" Shelly asked, and the teacher nodded. "Well, when I decide where I want to go with my portal pass prize, I was wondering . . ."

"Say no more, I'd love to be your virtual chaperone!" Leviathan exclaimed in a voice so loud that Newton swore he felt the floor shake a little under his feet.

"Thanks, Professor Leviathan." Shelly smiled.

"Okay, Monster Club, let me tell you what I've got for us today, because it's pretty exciting."

She picked up a glass vial from her desk. The students gathered around to get a closer look.

"Each one of these contains a nanochip," she said, "barely visible to the naked eye. They are based on microchip technology used to store identifying information about pets, in case they get lost. But I think we can find some more creative ways than that to program them, don't you?"

A murmur rose as everyone began to talk excitedly about the project.

"I knew you'd love this!" Leviathan said. "Great. I'd like everyone to work in teams. Newton, you can stick with Shelly, since you're new. But I'd like you two to work with Tootie."

"NO!" Tootie and Shelly blurted out.

Shelly blushed. "Sorry," she said. "It's just, you know that Tootie and I work differently, Professor. She likes to make big, scary monsters. And I like to help modify creatures to make their lives easier."

"Boring," Tootie muttered under her breath.

"Which is exactly why I want you to work together," Leviathan said. "You two can learn something from each other. Now, everyone pick a lab table. I've got some simple test subjects for you to work on."

Test subjects? Newton wondered what that meant—until he saw a butterfly in a small plastic container on their lab table. It had large black-and-yellow wings.

"*Papilo cresphontes,*" Shelly said. "Also known as a giant swallowtail. They live all over the island."

"Why is it called a giant?" Newton asked. "It's only about as big as my hand."

"Well, it's large for a butterfly," Shelly remarked. "Its wingspan can be as much as six inches."

Tootie took a seat and emptied the glass vial containing the nanochip into a round port on the computer.

"Let's get this party started," she said. She began typing, and a green glowing holographic image of the butterfly appeared in midair in front of her. "Why don't we make it *really* giant?"

She typed some more, and the holograph expanded to show a butterfly as big as Tootie. Newton jumped back.

"Whoa!" he cried.

"It doesn't look so pretty anymore," Shelly said.

Tootie kept typing. "And let's make it even scarier," she said. "How about fangs? And maybe neon orange and some spikes on its wings?"

Shelly quickly leaned forward, pressed a button on the keyboard, and the horrific holographic image disappeared. "That poor butterfly!" she said. "There's no reason to make it a hideous monster. We should use the nanochip to help it. Like, make it become invisible when a predator is near."

Tootie pretended to yawn. "What's the fun in that?" she asked.

"Well, Tootie," Shelly said, "my parents taught me that the *best* kind of science finds solutions to problems."

Tootie went back to her typing. "Who needs invisibility when you can have neon orange wings with spikes on them? Awesome!"

"That is ridiculous!" Shelly said. She turned to Newton. "I can't do this. We have to tell Professor Leviathan that we need a new partner."

Newton hesitated. He liked that Shelly wanted to do something good for the butterfly. But Tootie's plans for the butterfly were pretty impressive.

The fangs, the bright orange wings—they were the opposite of camouflage, the thing that he was able to do when he felt danger was near. It got him thinking.

What if I were like that butterfly? he wondered. *What if I got big and scary when I was scared?*

That's when the idea hit him. "Shelly, Tootie, what if you combine your ideas?" he asked.

"What do you mean?" Shelly asked.

"Well, maybe making the butterfly big and scary could help it, if a predator was near," Newton began. "Like, a bird might be afraid to eat it if the butterfly had fangs and spikes and stuff."

Shelly nodded slowly. "I see . . . so we could program the butterfly to become monstrous . . . but *only* when it's threatened by a predator."

Tootie nodded. "I could live with that."

"That might work," Shelly said. "But then how would the butterfly turn back to normal?"

"Well, we could program the chip to reverse the effect after thirty seconds," Tootie suggested. "Enough time to scare the predator away."

The two girls smiled at each other.

"So, did I come up with a good idea?" Newton asked.

"No," Shelly said. "A *great* idea!" She pulled up a chair next to Tootie. "Let's program this thing!"

Newton hung behind them, unsure of how to help. He didn't know anything about programming, or about most things, really. He had started high school with very little knowledge, and he didn't know why, since he mysteriously appeared at the school with significant memory loss and no idea where he came from. Still, he was a fast learner, and sometimes in class he felt like he understood everything clearly. And other times it was like he was learning for the first time.

He watched as Tootie and Shelly furiously typed code into the computer, programming the nanochip.

"This is pretty easy," Shelly said as they worked. "The nanochip comes with a basic code structure. We just have to fill it in."

Still, it took a few hours, and Newton's stomach rumbled. He was hungry—and a little bored, since Shelly and Tootie were doing all the work.

Just as he started thinking about dinnertime, Shelly turned to him. "It's ready! Newton, can you help us test it out?"

"Sure," Newton replied. "What do I have to do?"

Shelly handed him a butterfly net. "I'm going to implant the nanochip into the butterfly. Then we're going to set it free. You're going to chase it with the net. When it feels threatened, it will trigger the program."

Newton nodded. "I can do that."

Tootie's voice thundered through the classroom. "Professor Leviathan! We're ready for our experiment!"

The large teacher walked over to their lab table, and other students followed. Shelly had opened the butterfly container a crack and was gently injecting the nanochip with a needle.

"This will just pinch a little," she said soothingly. Then she looked up at Newton. "Ready?"

Newton nodded as he raised the butterfly net. "Ready!"

Shelly flung the lid of the container open. The butterfly fluttered out. Newton stepped toward it, waving the net.

"Hey, butterfly, come here," he said.

The butterfly calmly flew around the classroom, but it didn't change.

"Be meaner!" Tootie told him. "Growl, Newton!"

Newton clenched his teeth and stomped toward the butterfly. This time, he spoke in his loudest voice.

"I'm gonna get you!" he yelled.

The butterfly's movements got more and more frantic. Then, before everyone's eyes, it began to change.

It grew to the size of a large human. The yellow on its wings became neon orange, and spikes sprung from the wings' edges. Its front legs became two long, curved claws.

The butterfly's enormous black eyes fixed on Newton. It started to fly toward him. The wind from its massive wings was incredibly strong, which startled Newton. What was he to do next? As the butterfly came closer, he tried to stay calm.

"Easy now," Newton said. "This is just a demonstration!"

Whoosh! The monstrous butterfly swooped down on Newton. Its two claws grabbed him by the shoulders. Then it carried him away!

"Helllllp!" Newton yelled.

CHAPTER 3

Shiny in the Shadows

The giant butterfly carried Newton out of the classroom and down the hallways of the school. Students raced to get out of the way. They were used to seeing strange things at Franken-Sci High, but the students were still shocked to see a giant insect, and frantically tried to hide.

"It's just a butterfly!" Tootie told everyone as she and Shelly chased after them.

That didn't help.

"Don't worry, Newton!" Shelly called out. "The butterfly will return to normal in thirty seconds."

"Thirty seconds?" Tootie asked. "I thought you said thirty *minutes*!"

"You programmed the chip for thirty minutes?" Shelly wailed. "That's not good!"

"Whoooooaaaaa!" Newton screamed as the butterfly flew around a corner. Newton struggled to free himself

from the creature's grasp, but its grip was too tight.

Ahead, he could see the wide-open front doors of the school, leading out to the jungle. He imagined the butterfly carrying him out, over the trees, out across the Atlantic Ocean . . .

"Close that door!" Newton yelled.

Two students were standing by the door, talking. They looked up when Newton yelled, and their eyes got wide.

Then they ran.

"Nooooo! Close the door!" Newton cried.

The butterfly swooped toward the open door, and then . . .

Thump!

Newton suddenly fell to the ground. Dazed, he looked up.

The butterfly was back to its normal size. It flew out the door.

"That . . . was . . . close."

Professor Leviathan ran up, out of breath and panting. She held a small remote-control device in her hand. Shelly and Tootie caught up to her.

"I deactivated the nanochip," the professor wheezed. "I programmed remote deactivation abilities into all the chips, just in case things got out of control. I didn't expect that you two would create such a monstrous butterfly. Fast, too."

Shelly and Tootie looked at each other and dropped their heads.

"Good work!" Professor Leviathan said.

Shelly and Tootie broke into smiles then Shelly turned to Newton.

"Are you okay?" she asked.

Newton jumped to his feet. "I'm fine. That was kind of . . . fun. Almost."

"Let's go back to the lab and get our notes down," Shelly said.

Newton's stomach growled. "Mind if I get some dinner? I'm really hungry."

"No problem. I'm much too excited to eat," Shelly said. "I'll see you later!"

Shelly and Tootie walked off, congratulating themselves for their successful experiment as Newton hopped into the transport tube and was whisked off to the cafeteria.

It was late, and the cafeteria was almost empty. Newton quickly piled his plate with slices of spongy brown meat speckled with green and red bits.

He squinted at a sign over the entrée and asked the lunch lady, "What exactly is . . . Memory Enhanced Meatloaf?"

She leaned closer to him. "Well, it doesn't enhance your memory. It's just made from yesterday's burgers, so it's like a meatloaf enhanced with memories of being a burger. Get it?" she asked in a low voice. Then she shrugged. "Well, I tried. Mumtaz likes us to get all science-y with the food, but sometimes you just want to make meatloaf, you know?"

"Uh, sure," Newton said. He wasn't sure exactly what the cafeteria lady meant, but the food on his plate smelled good. He glanced around for Theremin and Higgy but couldn't find them, so he sat down at a table by himself.

As he finished wolfing down his meal, the lights in the cafeteria dimmed to indicate that dinnertime was over, and a small door opened in the wall beside Newton. Stubbins Crouch emerged and started cleaning the floor, riding atop a levitating sweeper. Newton nodded to the school custodian, then made his way out of the cafeteria.

Newton took the transport tube to the first floor and made his way down the hall.

That's when he felt it again. A prickle on the back of his neck. He stopped as he noticed a shadow spilling across the linoleum tiles on the wall.

Newton spun around.

Someone—he couldn't see who—ducked into a doorway.

Higgy, he thought, *this time I'm* sure *it's you.* It was time he turned the tables on his troublesome roommate. *I can get ahead of him!* he thought.

Newton charged over to the door leading to the basement and hurried down the stairs.

One lone, cage-covered light bulb hung from the ceiling, casting dim light everywhere. Newton ran down the corridor and around a corner. He kicked off his sneakers and socks and jumped up, latching on to the ceiling with his grippy fingers and feet. Then he waited. *When Higgy turns the corner, I'll jump down and scare him!* Newton thought, pleased with himself. He stayed still, waiting for Higgy to turn the corner, when he heard a familiar voice behind him.

"Roomie?"

He turned to see Higgy oozing out of a vent in the ceiling behind him! Startled, Newton dropped to the floor.

"Cheater!" Newton said. "I was going to scare you when you followed me down here. But you took the vent, and not the stairs."

"I wasn't following you," Higgy said.

"You don't have to lie," Newton told him. "I know it was you."

"Cross my gooey heart and hope to die, I swear it wasn't me," Higgy promised.

"Then who was it?" Newton asked.

As Higgy shrugged, they heard footsteps. Frowning, Newton quietly made his way back to the turn in the corridor, and Higgy followed him.

Someone was coming down the stairs. The glow from the light bulb made it impossible to see what the person looked like. In fact, Newton realized, the dim light seemed to reflect off the person's clothes—almost as though the clothes themselves were shiny.

"What do we do?" Higgy whispered.

"Let's lose him," Newton whispered back.

He and Higgy began to move through the underground maze of tunnels. Newton let Higgy lead the way. After all, Higgy knew the basement much better than Newton did, because Higgy liked to sneak around the school at night, searching for food to fill his always-hungry protoplasmic body.

They quickly made turn after turn, twisting and winding their way through the dark basement. They passed thick cobwebs, piles of discarded electrical devices, and moldy boxes containing jars filled with strange specimens. After five minutes, they stopped.

"I think we lost him," Newton said.

"Or her," Higgy added.

"Or it!" they said in unison.

"We don't know *what's* following you, really, do we?" Higgy asked.

"Good point," Newton said. He peered around a corner, followed by Higgy who extended one of his eyeballs on a green stalk.

Down at the end of the hallway, the figure was still approaching. Newton stifled a gasp and turned to Higgy.

"What now?" Newton asked.

"I think we need to step up our game, roomie," Higgy said as his eyeball rewound back into place. "Follow me!"

Higgy slinked up to the ceiling and climbed into a big metal air duct. Newton followed, using his grippy powers to climb up. They emerged onto the first floor, in front of the transport tube.

Whoosh! They got sucked up, but this time it didn't stop at the cafeteria. It stopped on the roof. It was a warm night, and the last remaining rays of the sun cast a soft yellow glow against the dark blue sky.

Then Higgy ran to the edge of the roof and started to ooze down the side of the building. Newton walked to the edge and looked down. It was a long drop to the ground—and a tiny part of his brain was telling him that he should be afraid, but the rest of his brain won out. With his grippy fingers and toes, it was easy for

Newton to climb down the side of the school building. When he reached the bottom, his feet touched soft grass.

"I hope whoever that was isn't still following us," Newton remarked.

"It would be highly unlikely," Higgy agreed.

"Let's get back to the dorms and really disappear," Newton said.

Higgy nodded, and they were headed toward the path when Newton had that prickly feeling again on the back of his neck.

Someone was sticking a leg out of one of the first-floor windows—someone wearing shiny pants.

"It's him, or it, or whatever!" Newton whispered to Higgy. Panicked, he ran back inside the school, and Higgy followed.

Newton recognized what he was feeling—Shelly would call it "freaked out." He'd felt like this before, when he'd used the Predictive Virtual Reality Goggles. And he didn't like the feeling one bit.

He ran up the stairs and into the first doorway he saw without really thinking—the entrance to the library. Inside, there were a few scattered students studying, reading holographic books, or having paper books delivered to them by new robotic conveyor belts that crisscrossed the large room. Instinctively, Newton

moved toward the bookshelves and stopped to catch his breath. Panting, he pressed himself up against the books.

That's when Higgy caught up to him.

"Newton?" he asked, looking around. "Newton?" Then he stopped and stared right at Newton. "Oh, *there* you are," he said. "Shelly said you had camouflage abilities. Most impressive."

"I'm doing it now?" Newton asked as he looked at his hands. He didn't feel any different at all.

Higgy nodded. "You're blending right in to that row of encyclopedias," he said. "Our pursuer will never find you."

"Can you see if we're still being followed?" Newton asked.

Higgy nodded. "On it."

Higgy flattened himself and slid underneath the shelves until he got to the end. Then he extended an eyeball out to scan the library.

"It's a guy, and he's wearing shiny pants!" Newton heard Higgy whisper.

"Can you see his face?" Newton asked.

"Let me get up a little higher," Higgy responded. "I just need to . . . ow!"

Newton jumped down from the bookshelf. "Higgy! Are you okay?"

Higgy slithered out from under the shelf. He had a hand over one eye.

"Somebody dropped a book on my eye," he whispered. "Sorry, I didn't get a good look at the guy."

A feeling of anger replaced the fear Newton had been feeling. "This has got to stop! Whoever it is, they can face me. Now!" he said.

Newton dashed out from between the bookshelves and into the central part of the library. There was nobody in shiny clothes in sight.

"I'm right here!" Newton called out as he looked around. "Whoever's following me, show yourself!"

A library drone instantly flew up to him. It hovered so close, Newton could see its metal clockworks whirring inside its plastic shell. It had helicopter-like propellers that whirred so quietly, the drones often startled anyone they approached.

"Quiet, please," it told Newton in a clipped mechanical voice. "Shhhhhhhhhhh."

"I know, I know," Newton said with a sigh. "Come on, Higgy, let's get out of here."

"Can we stop by the cafeteria?" Higgy asked as they left the library. "I've seen some amusing cartoons in which a cold, raw steak is used to help a black eye. My goo is still green, but I could give that a try. And then I could cook it and eat it."

"Sure, let's go," Newton said.

As they made their way to the transport tube, Newton looked around, hoping to see anyone in shiny clothes. Instead, he saw Theremin levitating down the hall, his eyes flashing angrily.

"Theremin! What's up?" Newton asked.

"I'm super upset with Father, that's what's up!" Theremin replied. "I got a message from Mumtaz that he *still* won't give me permission to use my portal pass!"

"That's not fair," Newton said.

"It's more than not fair!" Theremin replied. "And I'm going to find him and stand up to him for once!"

Determined, Theremin leaned forward and zoomed down the hallway. Newton and Higgy exchanged glances and took off after their robotic friend. Newton wanted to make sure that Theremin was going to be okay, of course, but he was also curious about meeting Theremin's dad.

Theremin angrily pushed through a door marked ROBOTICS LAB. Newton and Higgy followed him, narrowly avoiding getting hit by the heavy swinging door.

"Father! We need to talk!" Theremin yelled.

Dr. Rozika, a thin man with a head so bald it looked

like a polished egg, looked up from his work. "Lower your pitch and volume, Theremin. I am trying to concentrate," he said evenly.

Dr. Rozika's eyes were so cold and piercingly blue that they made Newton shiver. Robots in various stages of construction were carefully displayed throughout the lab.

"Why won't you let me use my portal pass?" Theremin said at a lower volume.

"Theremin," Dr. Rozika said coolly, "I made you intelligent enough to answer that question yourself."

"If that were true, I wouldn't be here," Theremin snapped.

Dr. Rozika sighed. "Well, if I must spell it out for you—as one of my most successful creations, I can't have you transporting out of this school to go who-knows-where."

"But I'll have a virtual chaperone," Theremin argued, then softened. "*You* could be my chaperone," Theremin lowered his voice even more, ". . . Dad."

Dr. Rozika frowned. "And take time away from my research? Don't be ridiculous, Theremin. Now run along with your little friends and leave me to my work."

Theremin's red eyes began to burn more brightly than before. Sparks sizzled from his metal head.

"Uh-oh," Newton said.

"I'm not a creation, I'm your SON!" Theremin yelled.

His head jerked to the right and two laser beams burst from his eyes, blasting one of the partially built robots. *Zap!* The robot's metal body began to glow, then melt, and become liquid.

"Theremin, enough!" Dr. Rozika scolded.

Zap! Zap! Zap! Theremin attacked the prototype robots one by one, turning them all into molten metal. Dr. Rozika calmly stood up and set his piercing eyes on Theremin.

"This is very disappointing, Theremin," he said, his voice like ice. "These robots you have just destroyed could have been your siblings. You should have known better. But I guess you're just not that smart after all."

"And whose fault is that?" Theremin asked. "You're the one who programmed me!"

As Theremin angrily glided out of the room, Newton and Higgy quickly followed. Newton had to run to catch up to his friend.

"You all right?" Newton asked.

"No!" Theremin snapped. "Didn't you hear? I'm stupid!"

Higgy reached them. "That was quite impressive, Theremin," he said.

Theremin stopped. He blinked. "Really?"

"Most definitely," Higgy said. "Excessive, yes, but still impressive."

"Yeah," Newton agreed. "You should be proud for standing up to your dad like that. He seems like kind of a . . ."

"*Jerk* is the word you're searching for." Theremin sighed. "A brilliant, award-winning jerk. And now he'll never give me permission to use my portal pass. I'll never know what it's like to sense the chilly feel of snow on my circuits."

"That might be a good thing," Higgy said. "Water and electrical circuits don't mix."

"I was going to wear a jacket!" Theremin insisted.

The three boys headed to the dorm. Newton couldn't help feeling sad for his friend. There had to be a way to help Theremin.

What was it his teachers always said? Newton would just have to use his *noodle noggin*!

CHAPTER 4

The Man with the Green Hair

"What exactly is this game again?" Newton asked Shelly the next day after school. "Coconut mess bull?"

Newton and Shelly were swept up in a crowd of students talking loudly as they streamed through the entrance to the school's stadium.

"Chrono-chess-ball," Shelly corrected him. "So, you have no memory of it?"

Newton shook his head. "Nope."

"It's based on three kinds of games: basketball, chess, and musical chairs," Shelly explained. "The players make goals with a ball while moving like pieces on a chess board. Besides moving side-to-side or forward-and-back, some can briefly move backward and forward in time!"

Newton nodded, trying to comprehend.

Shelly smiled. "And everyone cheers for their favorite team."

"Do we have a favorite team?" Newton asked.

"The Subatomic Scorchers," Shelly replied. "That's Theremin's team."

Newton scanned the students in the crowd. Some of them were wearing blue T-shirts or baseball hats with a lightning bolt on them. Others wore green fuzzy hats with monster ears.

"I get it," he said. "People dress up to show what team they like."

Shelly held up a blue flag with a white lightning bolt on it. "Or they hold signs or wave flags, like this one."

The ramp opened up to a large outdoor arena. Newton followed Shelly to the far side of the stadium where they found seats about halfway up the bleachers.

In the center of the stadium there was a giant chess board with squares big enough for students to stand on. On each side, a giant coil-shaped basket hung in the air.

"Good afternoon, students of Franken-Sci High!" a voice rang out. Suddenly, an enormous hologram of Ms. Mumtaz's head appeared in the center of the field.

"Today is a first-round match between the Subatomic Scorchers and the undefeated Megalithic Monsters," she continued. "May the best team win!"

The crowd erupted in cheers as the players ran out. The Subatomic Scorchers wore blue shirts with the white lightning bolt symbol on them, and blue shorts. The Megalithic Monsters wore green furry shirts with pants that looked like dinosaur legs.

The players on each team took their positions on opposite sides of the board and sat down on a spot.

Tootie Van der Flootin sat on the back row of the Monsters side.

"Why are they sitting down?" Newton asked.

"The positions are based on the pieces in a chess game," Shelly explained. "Tootie is the queen for the Monsters, and Rosalind Wu is the queen on the Scorchers side. That's why they're both wearing crowns."

"The players line up the same on both sides," Shelly went on. "Each team tries to protect their queen. Theremin is a knight. Just like in chess, the players can only move across the board in a specific way. Every time a player makes a move, he or she gets a chance to make a basket by throwing the chronoball into their team's coil at their end of the board. The more important the player, the more points they score. Pawns only earn one point. The game is played in four ten-minute quarters, and the team with the most points at the end wins. But if the ball hits the queen by mistake, one point gets deducted. And if the queen scores a basket, the game is over. Oh, and in every round, the players' starting positions on their team's side of the board are randomly shuffled according to a computer program, so there is always a new configuration."

"It sounds complicated," Newton admitted.

"Just watch. You'll get the hang of it," Shelly said.

Just then, Newton noticed that everybody was looking to the sky. A drone with a retracting metal claw flew over the field, clutching a round, glowing yellow-and-green ball that looked like it was filled with lightning or electricity. When it got to the middle of the field, the drone dropped the ball. Whoever caught it got to make the first move.

The stadium filled with cheers as one of the Monsters picked up the chronoball and made several zigzag moves toward the center of the board, and then tried to make a basket, but missed.

One of the Scorchers expertly caught the ball in one hand, but then Theremin scooped it up.

"Go, Theremin!" Newton cheered.

Theremin ducked and weaved around several Monsters and then chucked the chronoball. It flew out of his hand . . . hovered over the hoop . . . and then seemed to vanish as one of the Monster team members appeared out of thin air, jumped up, and knocked the ball away before it could go through the hoop!

"Where did he come from?" Newton asked, blinking his eyes in disbelief, as the kids in the Monsters bleachers jumped to their feet and let out a roar.

"The future," Shelly shrugged. "Rooks and bishops can travel back and forth through time for exactly three seconds using the chrono-wheels they're wearing. The Monsters rook must have seen Theremin score in the future—and went back in time to stop him."

"That is awesome . . . and confusing," Newton said.

Down on the board, Theremin didn't look awesome. His red eyes were flashing uncontrollably with anger. This was one robot who didn't like to lose.

"Uh-oh," Shelly said.

Theremin charged after the time-traveling rook, who was now carrying the ball, and tackled him.

Wham! The rook was slammed face-down into the board, hard. A referee drone with a black-and-white striped metal body and a swirling red light for a head hovered above Theremin.

"EXCESSIVE FORCE! EJECTED!" the drone declared.

"But I have super robot strength! I can't help it!" Theremin yelled.

"EJECTED! EJECTED!"

Three more referee drones appeared. They hoisted

Theremin off the ground and dropped him in a penalty box. The penalty was, in part, that his holographic image was projected onto the ceiling of the stadium so that everyone attending would see him pouting about his punishment.

"Poor Theremin," Shelly said. "He's never made it through a game. It's too bad, because he's a really good player."

Newton felt bad for Theremin, but he returned his attention to the field. The rest of the game was a blur as Scorchers and Monsters scored one after the other. In the final seconds of the fourth quarter, queen Tootie Van der Flootin lifted a Scorchers pawn holding the ball and lobbed them both into the hoop as the referee drones exclaimed:

"GAME OVER! GAME OVER! THE MONSTERS WIN 74–53!"

The Megalithic Monsters fans roared, the Subatomic Scorchers fans gasped, and Shelly and Newton went looking for Theremin. They found him sulking under a palm tree outside the stadium.

"It's not fair," he grumbled. "Chrono-chess-ball is antirobot. I can't help it if I knock players unconscious when I tackle them. I am made of metal, duh!"

"Maybe you could just not tackle them," Newton

suggested helpfully, but Theremin just scowled.

"Come on," Shelly said. She knew from experience that the best way to get Theremin out of a postgame funk was to distract him with gadgets and other toys. "Let's go to the Student Store. Maybe we can find something to cheer you up. Plus, we've never taken Newton there."

Theremin sighed. "Okay, but it's not going to change my mood."

Shelly was right—Newton had never been inside the school store before. He'd passed by it a few times, but he'd been so busy with classes and the Mad Science Fair that he didn't have time to explore.

The store was crowded with students who had stopped in after the chrono-chess-ball game. Newton looked around, wide-eyed. The stores shelves were stocked with fun-looking gadgets.

"Let's find the sample table," Shelly suggested, and the two boys followed her as she weaved through the crowd. She stopped at a levitating metal tabletop with a TRY ME sign on it and picked up a small spray can.

"Babel Breath Spray," she said. "Hmm. I wonder what this does?"

"I'll try it," Newton offered.

"You might as well," Theremin grumbled. "Robots don't have breath."

"Open wide!" Shelly said, and Newton opened his mouth. She pumped the spray and Newton felt a tingle inside his mouth.

"*Det smager frisk,*" Newton smacked his lips and smiled. Then he got a quizzical look on his face. "*Hvad sagde jeg bare sige?*"

"It broke his tongue!" Theremin cried as he pulled on Newton's hand. "We've got to take him to Nurse Bunsen!"

"*Ingen!*" Newton shook his head.

"I don't think that's it," Shelly said. "I think he's speaking another language."

"Which one?" Theremin asked.

Shelly pulled out her tablet, pressed a key, and held it up to Newton's face. "Say something."

"*Noget,*" Newton said.

"*Something,*" Shelly's tablet said aloud, translating Newton's speech into English. Shelly's eyes got wide. "You're speaking Danish! Cool!" she cried.

"*Ja!*" Newton agreed.

She picked up the can of Babel Breath Spray and squinted to read the fine print. "'One squirt allows you to speak another language for up to sixty seconds. Warning: Languages may differ with each spray.' Now that's kind of fun," Shelly said.

"*Ja, roligt! ROLIGT!*" Newton agreed.

"Hmph," Theremin snorted. "It's not very useful."

"That's why it's fun!" Shelly replied.

Theremin turned to a bin containing balls made of silver metal streamers. A sign overhead read: MAGNO-ELECTRIC ANTIGRAVITY POM-POMS!

"It would have helped to have someone cheering for me in today's game," Theremin said as he picked up a pair of pom-poms, shook them, and began to cheer:

"*Stronger than steel, brighter than the sun,
Theremin won't stop, 'cause he's number one!
GOOOOOOOO, THEREMIN!*"

As the robot held the pom-poms over his head, streaks of bright blue electricity snapped and crackled between them. Theremin was spun in place, then the pom-poms lifted him straight off the ground.

"Ahhhhhhhhhhhh!"

Theremin slammed into the ceiling as the pom-poms crashed through without him and kept shooting up, up, up, until they disappeared into the blue sky.

The robot fell to the floor, rolled over onto his back, and groaned. "Why does everything bad happen to me?"

"Theremin, that was way cool," Newton blurted out. Hearing his own voice, Newton touched his face. "Hey,

I've got my old voice back again!"

"Over here, guys," Shelly said, moving to another shelf. "Micro-Weather souvenir globes!"

She picked up a small clear dome. Inside, a tiny tornado twirled. "This one's a real tornado!" Even though the tornado was contained, Shelly's hair started being blown around as if she was inside it. She quickly put down the dome. "Maybe *too* real," she added.

Theremin moved to the shelf. He picked up one of the globes. "It's snow," he said. "Real snow!"

"Whoa. I've never seen snow either," Newton said. "At least, I don't think I have."

He stood closer to Theremin to get a better look inside the globe. Millions of tiny snowflakes were falling inside the globe, landing on the branches of a tiny forest of green trees. Suddenly, holographic snowflakes began to fall and swirl around Theremin!

"It's not the same as actually seeing snow with my portal pass, but it's better than nothing," Theremin said. "I'm gonna get it."

He made his way to the cashier—a bored-looking young woman with a large mechanical eyeball strapped across her forehead—and handed her the snow globe. She tilted her head, aimed the eyeball scanner at the globe, and then scanned Theremin's ID card.

The eyeball blinked rapidly, then a mechanical voice rang out. "REJECTED!"

"Impossible!" Theremin said. "I have a hundred allowance credits on my card."

The cashier shrugged as she pointed up to her eyeball headpiece. "It says you're rejected."

Theremin's eyes flashed red. "And I say it's a mistake!"

He took out his tablet and began typing. The holographic face of his father appeared.

"What is it now?" Dr. Rozika said with a sigh.

"Father! My ID card isn't working. My allowance credits aren't showing up," he said.

"There is nothing wrong with your card. I am withholding your allowance until the damage you caused to my lab is paid for," Dr. Rozika replied.

"Father!" Theremin wailed. "That could take forever!"

"Seventy-one years, four months, and eight days to be exact," Dr. Rozika replied. "Have a nice day, Theremin."

Dr. Rozika's face disappeared. Theremin's eyes began to flash.

Shelly could tell Theremin was about to lose it. She paid for the snow globe and gave it to Theremin. Then she grabbed Newton's arm. "Come on, we've got to get him out of here. There's too much valuable stuff he can destroy."

Shelly and Newton quickly ushered Theremin outside the shop.

"Come on, Theremin," Shelly said calmly. "Let's go to the dorms and try out your new snow globe there."

Theremin ignored her. "Father is so mean," he complained. "Why did he even create me in the first place?"

"Why don't you ask him?" Newton suggested.

"There's no point," Theremin mumbled as they stepped onto a sliding pathway that would carry them through an artificial rain forest and deposit them at the dorms.

"I'm sure he had a good . . . ," Newton began, then gasped as he felt the strange tingly feeling on the back of his neck again.

"Someone's following us!" Shelly yelled. "Over there!"

Newton spun around and saw a figure in shiny clothing duck behind a banana tree. Newton ran toward it, as Shelly and Theremin followed. But when they reached the tree and surrounded it, nobody was there!

"I've had enough of this!" Newton cried. "Some guy has been following me for days now! And the way he keeps disappearing is freaking me out!"

"It's not Higgy pranking you?" Shelly asked.

Newton shook his head. "He followed me and Higgy

yesterday. But we couldn't catch him then, either."

Theremin was concerned. "He might have been following us around the Student Store."

"Let's go to your room," Shelly said to Theremin.

"Why?" he asked.

"Because *you* just might have the answer!" Shelly replied.

A few minutes later the three friends stood in Theremin's dorm room. Newton thought that it was surprisingly neat. Theremin's metal sleeping pod had no blankets or pillows; the few clothes he wore fit neatly into the drawers of a plastic see-through dresser. A nearby shelf held specimens of rocks, jars of sand, and plant life that looked to Newton like they had been collected from the island.

Shelly turned out the light. "Theremin, scroll through your short-term memory circuits from when we got to the store. Maybe you accidentally recorded the guy who's following Newton."

"Sure," Theremin said as he faced the white wall. Bright beams of light shone from his eyes and projected a scene on the wall—the Student Store.

Newton realized that they were seeing everything that had happened in the Student Store from Theremin's point of view.

There was Shelly, spraying the Babel Breath Spray into Newton's mouth. Then Newton started talking, and Shelly laughed. Then the projection panned over to the bin of pom-poms. As they saw Theremin's hands reaching into the bin, there was a flash of shiny fabric on the far right side of the image.

"Stop!" Newton yelled, and Theremin froze the image.

Newton pointed. "See that arm there? That shiny sleeve? That's the guy who was following us."

"Zoom in and give us some slow-mo, Theremin," Shelly instructed.

The memory projection tightened to the mysterious image and moved forward, frame by frame, until the shiny sleeve was revealed to belong to a man in a shiny suit. The man had a wild head of green hair—and not just *any* green hair. It was so bright that it looked like it could glow in the dark.

"Pause it!" Newton cried. "This has gotta be the guy. Have either of you seen him before?"

Shelly shook her head. "He doesn't look familiar."

"I can access my facial recognition software," Theremin said. "I've got a personal database of every student and staff member in the school in my memory. Let me cross-check."

Newton heard whirring and clicking sounds coming from Theremin's head.

"Come on, Theremin," Newton whispered softly. "Who is it? Who is it?"

Then Theremin blinked, and the projected image faded. "He's not from Franken-Sci High."

"Hmm," Shelly said as she turned on the light. "Then who is he, and why is he following you, Newton?"

"I've been thinking about that," Newton said. "Remember when Mimi accused me of being a spy, trying to learn her family secrets? Well, maybe *she* sent someone to spy on me."

Shelly nodded. "It's possible. But if it's true, she didn't hire a very good one. What kind of spy goes around with bright green hair and shiny clothes?"

Newton sighed. "I guess that doesn't make sense," he admitted. Then something occurred to him. "What if he has something to do with my past? Maybe he knows who I am and where I'm from!"

"Anything's possible," Shelly said. He repeated the words in his head, and it felt good.

Anything's possible!

CHRONO-CHESS-BALL

Chrono-chess-ball is a combination of basketball, chess, and musical chairs, along with short-term time travel. It is played by two teams of sixteen players each. The game is played in four ten-minute quarters. The team with the most points wins.

Point Scoring and Special Rules

Each team has a specific number of players based on chess pieces. Different players earn different points for scoring a basket, which is made by throwing the ball into the coil:

8 pawns: Pawns earn 1 point when they score. Pawns can be eliminated from the game if they are hit with a ball from the opposing team.

2 rooks: Rooks earn 2 points when they score. A rook can use a chrono-wheel to travel back in time 3 seconds during any point in the game.

2 bishops: Bishops earn 3 points when they score. A bishop can use a chrono-wheel to travel forward in time 3 seconds during any point in the game.

2 knights: Knights earn 4 points when they score.

1 king: The king's main job is to protect the queen. A king earns 10 points when he scores.

1 queen: If a queen scores, the game ends, and the team with the highest points at that time automatically wins.

CHAPTER 5

The Obstacle Course of Doom

"Any sign of your shiny, green-haired mystery man today?" Shelly asked Newton the next morning. Newton, Shelly, and Theremin were walking through the school halls to their next class.

Newton shook his head. "Not yet, and I've been looking," he replied. Then he looked down at his tablet. "So, what's this new class that popped up on the schedule that we're going to? Phys Ed? Is that the name of a scientist?"

"It's short for Physics of Physical Education," Shelly replied. "We've always had the gym that any student can use in their free time, but this is the first time Phys Ed is an official class. Only a few professors were ever interested enough to teach it."

"Why?" Newton asked.

Shelly shrugged. "Maybe mad scientists are more into mental education than physical," she replied. "Anyway,

Mumtaz thinks it's important to be active."

"That's one good thing about being a robot," Theremin chimed in. He rapped on his metal body. "I'm fit as a fiddle, if that fiddle were made of metal! As a matter of fact, I'm exempt from the class."

"So why are you coming with us?" Newton asked.

"And miss the chance to see *other* kids humiliated, for once?" Theremin asked. "I wouldn't miss it!"

Newton started to feel nervous. "Humiliated?"

"I don't think it's what Mumtaz had in mind, but most of the classes involve tasks that no human can accomplish. You'll see . . . ," Theremin hinted.

"Don't worry, Newton, I'm sure you'll be fine," Shelly said. "We'll probably just do simple exercises and jog around a little."

But when they got to the gym, their jaws dropped. A massive structure had been erected. Rope bridges and hanging ropes led from one end of the gym to the next, suspended over giant glass tanks. One was a water tank that held sizzling, sparking, wriggling creatures. Another contained a swirling vortex.

"What is that?" Newton wondered out loud.

"It is an obstacle ropes course," said a mechanical voice next to him. "Don't you know anything, newbie?"

Newton turned to face Odifin Pinkwad—or rather,

Odifin Pinkwad's brain, since the unusual student was actually a brain floating in a jar of purple liquid. Odifin spoke through a speaker on the jar and was rolled around the school atop a metal table with wheels that was pushed by a skinny, slouching, greasy-haired teenager named Rotwang.

"I know some things, Odifin, but not everything," Newton informed him. "I still don't have my memory back."

"You're still sticking to that story, are you?" Odifin laughed. "Ha. Pathetic!"

Theremin glided between Odifin and Newton. "Why are you here, Odifin? You're exempt from gym, just like I am."

"I want to show that I'm superior, so Rotwang is going to participate for me," Odifin said, spinning his tank to indicate the teenager next to him, "as any well-trained personal lab assistant would."

"Right. What he said," Rotwang grunted.

The sound of a shrill whistle pierced the air. All eyes turned toward a six-year-old girl with red hair, wearing a white tracksuit and a whistle around her neck.

The gym teacher was Professor Juvinall.

"I almost forgot she was teaching this," Newton said. "I don't think she likes me very much."

"You mean because you called her a little kid," Theremin pointed out.

"But she *is*," Newton replied. "She's only six years old!"

Professor Juvinall blew her whistle again. "Quiet, everyone!" she yelled, in a voice that was exceptionally loud for a child. "Welcome to freshman level Phys Ed. I only ended up teaching this class because we drew straws, and I got the short one."

"That's because she *is* the short one," one of the students muttered. Juvinall's head snapped in the direction of the sound.

"Who said that?" she asked.

All the students froze. Nobody responded. Juvinall slowly turned to glare at Newton.

"Was it you, Warp?" she asked.

"N-n-no, Ms. Juvinall," Newton said nervously. "Not me."

Her green eyes narrowed. "It better not have been," she said. Then she addressed the class. "Okay, so to make things interesting, I personally designed this fun little course for this class. I call it the Obstacle Course of Doom."

Frantic whispers rose up from among the students.

"To be more accurate, you'll know it as the Ultimate,

Inescapable Obstacle Course of Death, Doom, and Destruction, and it's a beauty," Professor Juvinall said. "Designed to test your mental as well as your physical strength. Let me give you all a quick tour."

She pointed to a wall built with various contours. "First, you scale the Geometric Shapes Wall—where the triangles, squares, pentagons, and polygons will continuously change shape as you climb. Second, you grab any of those hanging tentacles and swing over the Electric Leech Lagoon." She paused and smiled. "They haven't eaten anything today."

Whimpers and gasps rose up from the students.

"Next, you run across the Sodium Bromide Bridge before it dissolves, jumping between the Matrix of Death Laser Beams as you go," Juvinall continued.

"*Death* lasers?" Newton whispered.

"Then you crawl your way through the Giant Web of Sticky Spider Silk," she said. "And *if* you don't get stuck, you'll come out on top of the Vortex Tank, where there is an escape hatch with a panel of buttons. To open the hatch, you'll see a sequence of flashing colored lights on the panel. You'll have twelve seconds to punch in the correct sequence. If you run out of time, a trapdoor will open and you'll drop into the center of the vortex, which will send you who-knows-where."

The gasps got louder.

"If you successfully cross the tank, your last challenge will be to jump down and hop through a line of inflatable pool toys," she said, pointing to lines of plastic pool toys of ducks, swans, unicorns, and dolphins at the end of the course.

"That last one seems kind of easy, doesn't it?" Theremin whispered.

"Shhh! Don't let her hear you," Shelly warned. "We don't need her to make this any harder!"

"So, is everyone ready to tackle the Ultimate, Inescapable Obstacle Course of Death, Doom, and Destruction?" Juvinall asked.

"Um . . . ready," the students mumbled cautiously, barely audible.

"Well, ready or not, we're starting!" she said. "The course can handle three victims—I mean, participants— at a time."

She looked down at her clipboard. "Up first: Rotwang on behalf of Odifin Pinkwad, Mimi Crowninshield, and Newton Warp!"

Newton looked at Shelly and Theremin, worried.

"You'll do great, Newton," Shelly said, but she sounded worried too. "I'm sure Professor Juvinall wouldn't let anything bad happen to any of us."

"I hope not," Newton muttered.

"Warp! Get over here!" the teacher barked.

Newton jogged over to the start of the course and stood between Mimi and Rotwang. Mimi cracked her knuckles and stared up at the imposing wall with a fierce look of determination in her blue eyes.

"Let's do this," she said.

"On my whistle," Juvinall said. "On your marks, get set . . ." *Tweet!*

Newton took off running and started to scramble up the Geometric Shapes Wall. From the corner of his eye he could see Mimi quickly moving up next to him. Rotwang was so tall that he easily scrambled to the top of the wall and pulled himself up.

By the time Newton reached the top of the wall, Rotwang was already holding on to a tentacle and swinging across the water tank. His long legs splashed against the water, and the electric leeches snapped at his ankles with their tiny toothy mouths.

Good thing I've got extra-grippy fingers! Newton thought. He took a deep breath, grabbed on to a tentacle, and swung himself across the pool. He could hear cheering in the background. *"Go, Newton! You can do it!"*

He landed on the other side of the tank with a thud.

In front of him, Rotwang had already begun to race across the Sodium Bromide Bridge, which was starting to bubble and dissolve. His feet were so big that he kept hitting the Death Laser Beams.

"Ow! Ow! Ow!" Rotwang yelped, and slowly made his way across.

Danger! Danger! Danger! Newton's brain screamed at him, and he couldn't move. Luckily, his camouflage instinct didn't kick in, either, which would have meant everyone in class would know his special skill.

That's when Mimi caught up to him. "What are you just standing there for, Newton? Scared?"

Newton blinked. He hadn't realized he was frozen in place until he heard Mimi's voice. The very thought of Death Laser Beams had paralyzed him with fear.

"No, I'm not scared!" he said, trying to sound convincing. Mimi just laughed and began to hop and skip across the bridge, expertly avoiding the Death Lasers Beams. When she was in the middle, she looked back at Newton triumphantly.

"I was elementary school hopscotch champion for three years in a row!" she said. Then she turned and kept hopping across, getting closer to Rotwang and the tangled Giant Web of Sticky Spider Silk.

Newton snapped out of his stupor when he heard

Theremin cheering from the gym floor below.

"Stronger than steel, brighter than the sun,
Newton won't stop, 'cause he's number one!
GOOOOOOOO, NEWTON!"

Newton smiled and stepped onto the bridge. He scanned the pattern of lasers and cautiously took his first hop.

He expected to feel the pain of a laser, but instead his foot landed safely. More confident now, he quickly hopped across the bridge and then jumped onto the Giant Web of Sticky Spider Silk, relieved to have made it across.

Newton had expected Mimi and Rotwang to be far ahead of him but was surprised to see Rotwang's gangly legs and arms completely tangled up in the sticky mesh. And Mimi was climbing hand-over-hand along the bottom of the web, in a shouting match with Odifin.

"Just give up now, Mimi!" Odifin taunted her through the speaker on his jar. "You'll never make it all the way across!"

Mimi held on to the sticky webbing with one hand as she looked down and shook her fist at Odifin.

"Stuff it, pickled brain!" Mimi yelled. "At least I'm not tangled up like your dopey assistant!"

Newton knew Odifin was just trying to shake Mimi's confidence. He tried to ignore them and began to crawl through the web. The spider silk swayed as he grabbed each strand, but once again his grippy hands kept him steady. Mimi didn't even notice as Newton easily made his way past her.

"Rotwang might be dopey, but at least he's not some silly girl!" Odifin yelled at Mimi.

Mimi's eyes flashed with anger. "What did you say?"

"I said there's no way a *girl* is going to beat me, I mean, Rotwang!" Odifin shot back.

Mimi let go of the web and dropped to the floor. She charged toward Odifin, fuming.

"How *dare* you!" she yelled. "Girls can do anything boys can do!"

Professor Juvinall blew her whistle. "On the bench, Mimi! You're disqualified!"

"You can't do that!" Mimi protested. "I'll tell my parents!"

Newton tried to ignore the drama going on below him and finish the course. By now Rotwang had miraculously untangled himself and was standing on top of the Vortex Tank. As Newton climbed closer to the tank, he focused on keeping his balance while keeping an eye on Rotwang.

A control panel in front of Rotwang had rows of buttons that lit up in six different colors: red, blue, yellow, green, orange, and purple. The lights blinked

quickly in a random sequence.

Red, red, blue, purple, orange, green, red, green, yellow, blue.

"It's easy, Rotwang, repeat the sequence!" Odifin called up to him.

"Twelve seconds!" Professor Juvinall yelled.

The control panel began to beep out the seconds.

Beep. Beep. Beep.

Rotwang stared at the buttons, scratching his head.

"Rotwang, you oaf!" Odifin yelled.

Beep. Beep. Beep.

Rotwang began randomly pressing buttons.

Blue, purple, orange, orange, yellow, red, red, green.

"No, no, you brainless flatworm!" Odifin yelled.

Frustrated, Rotwang started pounding the buttons with his fist.

Beep. Beep. Beep.

"It's as simple as quantum addition!" Odifin screamed. "Red, red, blue, purple, orange, green, red, green, yellow, blue!"

Beep!

Rotwang smiled, wiggled his index finger, and slowly lowered it to the panel.

Beep!

BEEEEEEEEEEEEEP!

At the sound of the last beep, a trapdoor opened beneath Rotwang and he fell into the swirling vortex. "Master!" he yelled.

"Rotwang!" Odifin cried as his dutiful assistant disappeared.

The trapdoor slammed closed and Newton stepped up to the flashing light display.

"Concentrate, Newton!" Shelly yelled up at him.

He took a deep breath and watched carefully as the lights flashed.

Green, yellow, yellow, blue, purple, orange, red, yellow, green, orange.

The timer began its countdown.

Beep! Beep!

Newton started pressing buttons. Somehow, he remembered the sequence. He didn't know how he was doing it, but he didn't have time to think about it.

Green. Yellow. Yellow. Blue. Purple. Orange. Red.

Then he stopped and stared. What had come after the red? Was it yellow, green, orange? Or green, yellow, orange?

Beep! Beep! Beep!

Newton started to sweat. His mind was suddenly blank. Panic was setting in but he had to try. He pressed three more buttons.

Green. Yellow. Orange.

Nothing happened. He must have gotten something wrong. At least he had time to start over.

Beep! Beep! Beep!

He quickly started pressing again. *Green. Yellow. Yellow. Blue. Purple. Orange.*

Newton hesitated. What came next?

That's when he heard it—a strange voice calling up from below. "Newton Warp! Use your *noodle noggin!*" Newton didn't recognize the voice, but when he heard those words, something clicked in his brain.

Beep! Beep!

He remembered. It was so simple! *Red. Yellow. Green. Orange.*

Beep!

The panel of buttons flipped open to reveal the escape hatch.

BEEEEEEEEEEEEEP!

Newton jumped into the escape hatch and slid to safety just as the trapdoor dropped open. He could hear cheers from the students below.

He jumped to the floor and began to hop through the line of inflatable pool toys. He hopped faster as he reached the swan toys and then the unicorns. He was steps away from the dolphin toys when he heard the cheering grow louder and louder. Newton turned to look at the crowd, not because of the cheering but because of that familiar tingling on his neck. That's when he saw it. A head of green hair! Startled, Newton tripped over the horn of a unicorn pool toy and fell flat on his face.

The crowd gasped.

"On your feet, Warp!" Professor Juvinall growled. "Move it, MOVE IT!"

Newton jumped up and looked behind him. There was no sign of the green-haired man anywhere. Newton finished hopping through the dolphin toys and was heading for the finish line when a deafening sound roared into the gym.

Newton—and everyone else—looked up. A second whirling vortex opened up in the gym ceiling and Rotwang came tumbling out, his lanky limbs flailing, and landed on the gym floor next to Odifin with a thud.

"Rotwang," Odifin shouted. "You came back!"

Rotwang didn't have time to answer, because the roaring vortex began to suck up the obstacle course. Strands of the web streamed up through the air, wriggling like snakes. Students began to scream and run.

"Class dismissed!" Juvinall yelled as the vortex pulled her whistle off her neck.

Newton ran to the nearest exit and slammed the door

behind him, puffing and panting. Shelly and Theremin pushed their way through the crowd in the hallway and found him.

"You did great back there!" Theremin yelled over the noise.

"Thanks!" Newton replied. "But I didn't get to finish."

"Well, I'm glad I never had to start!" Shelly said. "That vortex was no joke."

Newton nodded. The three friends ran down a staircase and stopped at the bottom to catch their breath. Newton nervously looked from side to side.

"Do you think you're being followed again?" Shelly asked.

"Yes," Newton replied. "I saw the man with the green hair in the gym!"

CHAPTER 6

Who Is Dr. Flubitus?

"Why are we going to Yuptuka's class?" Theremin asked, as he, Newton, and Shelly made their way there. "I thought she was still stuck on the moon."

"They got a substitute teacher," Shelly replied.

"Well, whoever it is, I hope they're not as spacey as Yuptuka," Theremin said.

When they entered the classroom and sat down, Newton's seat was behind Mimi. She turned around to talk to him.

"Nice work on the obstacle course back there, Newton," Mimi said. "Of course, I would have beaten you if Odifin hadn't opened his big mouth."

"Well, technically, he doesn't have a mouth," Newton pointed out. "He's a brain in a jar."

Mimi frowned. "You know what I mean!" she snapped. Then she turned around.

The bell rang to announce the start of class, but there

was no teacher in sight. The kids stayed quiet for a minute. Then everybody started talking.

"This is ridiculous!" Mimi said. "There's no substitute. We should just get up and leave."

A murmur of agreement rose up from the students. Newton looked to Shelly and Theremin and made a "what now?" gesture. Then a voice made him turn around.

"Salutations, students!"

A tall man confidentially strode into the room—and promptly tripped and fell! He wasn't hurt, but he had dropped the load of folders he was carrying, spilling papers all over the floor.

Some of the kids giggled at the man's clothes as he got to his feet. He wore shiny black pants, yellow rubber boots, a yellow shirt with barely visible purple polka dots, a black vest striped with LED lights, and a red bowtie. A tight-fitting bowler hat was pulled down to the top of his ears.

The strange man took a few steps and walked straight into his desk. Then he turned, faced the wall-size digital screen, and cleared his throat.

"As I was saying . . . salutations, class!" he bowed to the screen.

Laughter rose up from the students.

"Um, sir, we're behind you," Shelly said helpfully.

The man spun on his heels. "Of course you are!" he announced. He put his index fingers to his eyes. "I've got my night-vision contacts in, but as you probably know, it's daytime, so I can't see very well at all. Goodness, I swore last time would be the, well, last time."

He took out the contact lenses, pulled a case from of his vest pocket, and popped them inside. Then he turned the case over, opened it, and popped two new lenses into his eyes.

"Ah yes, I lost my regular contacts, so these wavelength visualizers will have to do," he mumbled, apparently to himself. "Not ideal for a classroom situation, but I mustn't hold up your education!"

He cleared his throat again. "Young seekers of knowledge and know-how, it is I, Dr. Hercule Flubitus, here to instruct you in Dimensional and Interdimensional Teleportation from now on, hopefully, if all goes well."

The strange man then dramatically whipped off his hat—revealing a head of wild, bright green hair!

Newton gasped loudly. He whipped his head around to look at Shelly and Theremin. Both were wide-eyed.

The professor was the man in Theremin's footage! The man who had been following Newton around campus! *But why would a new professor be following me around?* Newton wondered.

"Now, I've got an exciting lesson planned for you today," Flubitus said as he held up his hand. He looked to see that the hand was empty. "Oh dear. Where did it go?"

"Do you mean those papers on the floor?" someone called out.

"Yes, yes, positively—the papers!" Flubitus said. He walked over to the fallen papers—and then slipped on them and toppled backward, his arms flailing.

Shelly jumped up to help him, and Newton followed her—partly out of curiosity, and partly because he knew Shelly was a good person and he wanted to follow her lead.

The two of them helped Dr. Flubitus to his feet. Newton searched the professor's face for some kind of reaction to seeing him, but Dr. Flubitus acted like he didn't know Newton at all. Then they helped pick up the papers and stuff them back into the folders. Most of the papers were covered with scribbled writing, symbols and numbers that Newton could barely decipher as being in English. And one was covered with lines of computer-generated bar codes.

"Many thanks," Dr. Flubitus said as he took the folders from Shelly and Newton and carefully made his way to his desk—safely, this time.

"Today we're going to discuss . . . ," he began as he randomly pulled a page from a folder, "the physics involved with dimensional teleportation!" He squinted at the paper. "One cup of chocolate chips. One half-cup of jellybeans. Two and a half eggs. Two cups of flour."

"Professor?" Mimi said as her hand flew into the air.

"Sorry," Flubitus said, "have I lost you already?"

"That sounds like a cookie recipe!" Shelly answered.

Dr. Flubitus froze in place. He blinked. "Cookie?" He looked at the paper and then sniffed it. "Why yes, you're correct. My aunt Venitis makes the *best* jellybean chocolate cookies."

The professor shuffled through his papers, muttering, "Just give me a second," then he smiled and raised an index finger, "which happens to be 1/86,400th of a mean solar day."

The students stared at him blankly, so he returned to his search. "I'm sure I'll find what I'm looking for. It's a bit hard to see much with the wavelengths oscillating as they do."

Restless, the students in the class started to whisper to one another.

"I've heard of this guy," Gustav Goddard said. "He's from a family of mutants; that's why he has green hair."

"You're wrong," said Tabitha Talos. "I heard that he

is descended from a tribe of sentient broccoli warriors."

"Well, I know exactly who he is," Mimi said with certainty. "Dr. Flubitus approached my parents about using the newest invention designed by Crowninshield Corporation: a human cloning device. Of course they refused, so he's probably here to try to get to my parents through *me*!"

Newton thought about this. Mimi was always bragging, and she was a very suspicious person. She probably still thought that Newton was a spy trying to steal her family's secrets. So, her suspicions might be true, he realized, but something was still not right.

"Why wouldn't your parents sell him the device?" Newton asked.

"It's still in the prototype phase," Mimi replied. "They didn't even know how Flubitus found out about it. He asked for early access—probably so he could steal the technology and sell copies of it!"

"Ha!" Theremin laughed. "Copies of a cloning device. Funny."

Shelly motioned to Newton and he scooted his chair closer to her. Theremin leaned in to listen too.

"Mimi's story is interesting, but it doesn't explain why Flubitus was following you," she whispered. "We should talk about this."

Newton nodded. "Yeah."

"Let's meet in my lab after class," she suggested.

For the rest of the class, Dr. Flubitus rummaged through his papers and muttered to himself while his students whispered, doodled, and napped. Finally, he gave a shout.

"Eureka!" he cried as he held a sheet aloft. "The basic mathematical principles of dimensional transportation. Number one—"

Ding!

The end-of-class bell rang, and the classroom door opened as everyone jumped up from their seats.

"We'll have a test about today's class on Thursday!" Dr. Flubitus called out, as everyone streamed from the classroom. "Or is the next class on Friday? Hmm. Well, be prepared for a pop quiz, sometime around Thursday-ish, but I'm just not certain. The universe and time are a mystery, indeed!"

Shelly, Newton, and Theremin made their way to the building's basement, to Shelly's animal rescue lab.

"Hello, Shelly! Hello, Shelly!" said a flying miniature dinosaur that squawked like a parrot and had robotic wings. It flew over to Shelly and landed on her shoulder.

"Hello, Wingold," she said, smiling. "You're looking good today."

"*Looking good!*" Wingold repeated.

Shelley walked up to a glass tank and picked up a jar next to it. Then she lifted the lid of the tank and started sprinkling in the contents of the jar—what looked like bugs to Newton.

"Here you go, Kermie. It's soy cricket time!" Shelly said.

The inhabitant of the tank, a frog with two springs for back legs, hopped up to the imitation crickets and gobbled them up.

"See? Those cruelty-free crickets are tasty, aren't they?" Shelly asked the frog. Then she motioned for Theremin and Newton to join her at the small round table in the center of the lab.

"Okay, let's talk about Flubitus," Shelly said.

"WAIT!" Newton cried as he jumped up and ran to the door. He quickly scanned the hall, then closed the door and locked it.

"For all we know, he's still following me," Newton said, sitting back down.

"Newton, are you sure that Flubitus has been following you and not *all* of us?" Shelly asked. "One time he did follow you *and* Higgy, right?"

Newton thought about it. "Yes, but other times I was by myself," he replied. "So, I'm pretty sure it's me he's after. I've got a . . . gut feeling."

"So, what does he want with Newton?" Theremin asked.

Shelly shrugged. "I'm not sure. If Mimi is telling the truth about the cloning machine, then I don't understand why Flubitus would be following Newton instead of Mimi."

"I'll give her a lie detector test," Theremin offered, rubbing his metallic hands together. "Father recently upgraded my extendible truth sensors."

"I don't think Mimi would let you do that," Newton said.

"Not in a million millenniums," Shelly said with a thoughtful frown. "Maybe we should tell Mumtaz about this."

"Forget Mumtaz," Theremin said. "Let's just march right up to Flubitus and ask him why he's following Newton!"

Newton hesitated. "I . . . I don't know. I'm pretty sure that Flubitus is the guy who's been following me. But what if it's just a coincidence that Theremin caught him on camera? Maybe we need to know more first."

Shelly nodded. "We can try to get more information first, sure," she said. "I mean, Flubitus is so weird he couldn't possibly be dangerous."

"Yeah, he's kind of a goofball," Theremin agreed.

"So, let's keep our eyes open and see what we've found by the weekend," Shelly said. "Although, this weekend Newton is supposed to take his portal pass trip."

"That's right!" Newton said, suddenly remembering. "And once I get home to my family, I mean—who knows? I might not even come back here."

Shelly and Theremin were quiet when he said this, and then reality hit Newton, too. If he *did* find his family this weekend, they might want him to stay with them and go to school wherever they live. He might learn that he was never supposed to come to Franken-Sci High in the first place.

And that meant—Newton might never see Shelly and Theremin again.

The truth suddenly sank in for the three friends.

"If that happens, I'll miss you," Shelly said.

"Yeah. Me too," said Theremin.

"Not as much as I'd miss you guys," Newton said. "I mean, right now *you're* my family."

"Well, even if you do end up far away, we can still be friends," Shelly said. "We can send holograph videos to each other."

"Speak for yourself," Theremin said. "Computer cameras make my face look fat."

Newton laughed. "Yeah, you're right!"

Theremin blinked. "I didn't mean for you to agree with me."

"Just kidding," Newton smiled. "And even if I *do* find my family, it doesn't mean we have to stop being friends."

The strange problem with Professor Flubitus suddenly became unimportant. Newton was going to stay focused on a more important goal: In just a few days, he was going to find out where he came from!

CHAPTER 7

Portal Pressure!

Over the next few days, Newton could barely contain his excitement about being able to use his portal pass soon.

He thought about the portal during Dark Matter Matters class, and Professor Phlegm gave him ten demerits for not paying attention.

He thought about the portal during his Advanced Emotional Chemistry class, and just couldn't get his sadness formula to work—all because he was too happy to care.

He thought about the portal during History of Mad Scientists class, which was easy to do because Professor Wagg—who was 115 years old—slept through most of the class, giving his students a lot of free time for extra activities.

He even thought about the portal while he planned a little "surprise" for Theremin, with the help of Higgy.

And then, finally, Saturday morning dawned. Newton

sprang out of bed early—so early that he bumped into
Woller in the hallway after he was already awake and
dressed.

"*Ca-wee! Ca-wee!*" the winged monster squealed.

"Save it, Woller," Newton said. "I'm awake and ready
to go!"

When he stepped outside, Shelly and Theremin were waiting for him.

"I am so excited!" Newton grinned.

"Yeah, well . . . we're excited for you too," Theremin mumbled in a flat voice.

Newton had asked his friends to see him off on his journey, but he hadn't thought about how it might be hard for Theremin. Dr. Rozika still hadn't given Theremin permission to go.

"I'm sorry you can't use your portal pass, Theremin," Newton said.

"It stinks," Theremin agreed. "But I guess I'm happy for you, anyway."

"Thanks, pal." Newton smiled weakly.

They made their way to the administrative building.

"So, Mumtaz said she'll be my chaperone," Newton said as they walked. "And she's going to explain how the pass works, too."

"It's easy," Shelly assured him. "You've been practicing folding the brochure. And once you have a pass, you'll get where you're going in a flash."

"Does it hurt at all?" Newton asked.

Shelly shook her head. "You won't feel a thing."

When they reached the door of the headmistress's office, Theremin knocked.

"Come in!" Mumtaz instructed.

When they entered, they found the headmistress standing there—or rather, a hologram of the headmistress, flickering next to her desk.

"Good morning, Newton!" she said. "Since I'm going to be your chaperone, I thought I might as well project from my room, instead of my office, so I can stay comfy."

She lifted up one foot to reveal that she was wearing fuzzy slippers.

"Sure," Newton said. "So, um, what do I do?"

"You have your brochure with you?" Mumtaz asked. Newton nodded and patted his shirt pocket. "Good. Now for your portal pass."

She raised a holographic remote and pressed a button. A door slid open on the top of her desk and a mechanical hand emerged clutching a small golden card.

Newton's eyes widened as he stared at the prized portal pass. It shimmered with the Franken-Sci High logo embossed on it.

"Next, you must properly fold the brochure. I'm sure you've been practicing?" Mumtaz asked.

"Every day," Newton smiled.

Newton took a thin pair of gloves from his pants pocket and slipped them on. The key to opening the

portal was to fold the metallic brochure in a very complicated way. His grippy fingertips had made it impossible to fold the portal correctly the first few times he'd tried. Only when Shelly had suggested the gloves was he finally able to do it correctly.

Shelly leaned in to Newton. "You've got this, Newton!" she whispered.

Newton then took the brochure from his shirt pocket and placed it on Mumtaz's desk. He opened it fully, into the shape of a big square. Then he bent in each corner so that they met in the middle, making a smaller square. Then he turned it counterclockwise and folded that square in half. And then in half again. Finally, Newton gave the brochure a quarter turn to the right then folded it diagonally so that the top left corner and bottom right corners touched.

Suddenly, the tightly folded brochure began spinning in place, then slowly lifted off the desk. As it swirled faster and faster in front of Newton, it created a rotating column of air that expanded to engulf the desk and Newton. The spinning column scattered the papers on Mumtaz's desk all around the room.

The swirling column began to blur and then the folded brochure vanished and was replaced by a human-size hole directly in front of Newton. The outline of the hole pulsed with a bright light, but when Newton peered into it, all he could see was black.

Then he heard Mumtaz's voice.

"Holding the portal pass in your left hand, say where you want to go," she instructed.

Newton grabbed the pass, gripped it tightly, and took a deep breath.

The moment had come. He had practiced it over and over in his mind for days. And now it was really happening. It was finally time to say . . .

"I want to go home!" Newton cried.

"Jump!" Mumtaz's holograph said.

Newton jumped into the hole. The blackness engulfed him. His skin tingled. His hair stood on end. He felt weightless, like he was tumbling head over heels in space. Colored lights swirled and twirled around him.

Then . . . *whomp!* Newton's feet landed on solid ground. The portal winked out as the folded brochure reappeared, then dropped to the ground. The blackness faded. Newton blinked as his heart pounded. He was home!

As his eyes adjusted, Newton saw the hologram of Mumtaz in front of him—flanked by Shelly and Theremin. Puzzled, he looked down to see the floor of the headmistress's office. Papers were still scattered all about. He looked around, frantic and disappointed.

"No, NO . . . I'm still here!" he cried. "It didn't work!"

"Maybe you misfolded?" Theremin asked.

"But I didn't!" Newton said.

"I saw it, you *did* fold the brochure correctly," Mumtaz agreed. "It could just be a glitch. It's been known to happen."

"Can he try it again?" Shelly asked.

"Certainly," Mumtaz said.

Newton picked up the brochure and expertly folded it again. The swirling portal appeared. He held the portal pass firmly in his left hand.

"Take—me—*home*!" he yelled.

Newton jumped into the portal. He felt the same sensations as before. Then the portal spit him out . . . right back into Mumtaz's office.

Newton almost felt like crying. "What's wrong, Ms. Mumtaz?"

"Well, perhaps there's a problem in Rome," Mumtaz said.

"Rome?" Newton asked. "What does that have to do with anything?"

"That's where you said you wanted to go, isn't it?" she asked.

Newton shook his head. "No, home. I said I wanted to go *home*."

A dark, sad look crossed the headmistress's face. "Oh, this hologram connection must be bad." Then she quickly recovered and put on her best smile. "No bother. Glitches do happen, you know," she said quickly. "Even at Franken-Sci High. Sorry it didn't work out, Newton. Just leave the portal pass on my desk and I'll have a look at it Monday. Have a nice weekend!"

"But—" Newton began, but Mumtaz's hologram was gone.

Newton sighed. "Now what am I supposed to do?"

Theremin put an arm around him. "Sorry, pal. Looks like both of us are members of the stuck-at-school club!"

"Don't give up hope!" Shelly pleaded. "With Mumtaz helping you, I bet it'll get fixed and you'll be home soon. At least you know where you want to go . . . I can't decide."

"I hope you're right," Newton said. He reluctantly placed his portal pass on the desk and with a sigh, left the office.

What if I never find out where I'm from? he wondered.

CHAPTER 8

Monster on the Loose

Newton could only stare down at his feet as he, Shelly, and Theremin left Mumtaz's office.

"Hey, let's get something to eat," Shelly suggested. "We were so excited about your portal pass that we forgot breakfast."

Newton shrugged. "Sure. Whatever."

When they reached the elevator tube, Newton frowned. "Can we take the stairs? I'm still kinda woozy from the portal."

"Whatever you want, Newton," Shelly said.

They made their way up the staircase, a spiral of metal stairs that went from the first to the last floors. Although it was Saturday, there were still students in the halls, heading to study groups, club meetings, or getting a snack in the cafeteria.

"This is easy for me," Theremin said as they climbed up the twisty stairs. "That's one of the benefits of being a robot that levitates. No calf muscles."

Normally Newton would have laughed at his friend, but he couldn't muster a smile.

When they reached the second-floor landing, a scream shook Newton from his gloomy thoughts.

"MONSTER!"

Newton turned to see Odifin Pinkwad, sloshing around inside his jar, zooming around a corner and then down the hallway toward them on his wheeled table, being pushed by Rotwang. The teenaged assistant looked shaken. They zipped right past the three friends and kept going.

"MONSTERRRRRRRRRR!" Odifin shouted.

"Nice try, but you can't scare us!" Theremin called after him, then grunted. "That was so silly."

"What do you mean?" Newton asked. "How do you know he was just pranking us?"

"Monsters are no big deal around here," Shelly chuckled. "Nobody at Franken-Sci High is scared of them. Besides, you don't see anybody else screaming, do you?"

"MONSTER!"

Two more students ran around the corner, frightened. They were followed by a crowd of kids that charged past Newton, Shelly, and Theremin and down the hall.

"Then again . . . ," Shelly said. "Maybe we should check this out."

She ran in the opposite direction of the panicked crowd, and Newton and Theremin followed her. When they turned the corner, there was no monster in sight.

"False alarm," Theremin said.

"Definitely," Newton agreed.

"Then let's head up to the cafeteria," Shelly suggested. "Maybe somebody knows what's going on."

They climbed up two more flights of stairs and found a group of frightened kids talking in the cafeteria.

"I saw it! It was terrifying!" one kid was saying.

"Are you talking about a monster?" Shelly asked.

The kid nodded. "It came out of nowhere! It was huge! It had huge fangs!"

"And flame-throwing claws!" another added.

"And a hundred insect legs!' another kid cried.

Newton looked at Shelly. "That sounds pretty scary."

"Yeah," Shelly said as she stared past Newton and Theremin. "And who do we know who likes to make big, scary monsters?"

Newton followed her gaze across the cafeteria. It landed on Tootie, who was sitting by herself and eating a stack of Extreme Pancakes. They approached her.

"Tootie, have you heard about this monster everyone's talking about?" Shelly asked.

"You bet!" Tootie nodded. "Doesn't it sound awesome?"

"Come on, you can tell us," Shelly said. "You created it, right?

Tootie looked at Shelly blankly.

"Did you tinker with a microchip," Shelly continued, "and turn a tadpole or a bedbug into a hideous beast? And then let it loose?"

"No way," Tootie said. "I only wish it was me!"

Theremin leaned toward her. "Then you won't mind if I use my lie-detector truth sensors on you?"

Tootie shrugged. "Go ahead." She held out her hands. "But what's the big deal if I am lying?"

"Because," Shelly said, "the technology that Professor Leviathan uses is supposed to be for helping animals, not creating scary creatures for fun."

"Do you really think I would invent a terrifying monster and then release it on campus?" Tootie sniffed. She sounded hurt. Then she shrugged. "Sure, there was that one time when the Snack Shack was squished, but I took really good care of the monster I made for my Mad Science Fair project. I kept it on a leash and everything!"

"I guess I believe you," Shelly sighed, but she didn't sound convinced.

Tootie stood up and held her hands out again. "Then test me, Theremin. I'll prove it to all of you."

"Goody," Theremin said. He faced Tootie.

Panels on each side of the robot's head opened up, and two wiry mechanical arms sprang out. Cuffs at the end of each arm gripped Tootie's wrists.

Theremin's eyes became swirling black spirals as he stared at Tootie.

"Tootie Van der Flootin?" he asked. "Look into my eyes and hear only my voice."

"Sure thing, Theremin," she said.

A green beam of light shot from Theremin's eyes and locked onto Tootie's eyes.

"Now tell me that you didn't create this new monster," Theremin instructed.

"I did not create this new monster," Tootie repeated calmly.

Beeps and whirring sound came from inside his head. Then suddenly, the two mechanical arms released Tootie's wrists and snapped back inside Theremin's head.

Shelly leaned into Theremin. "Well?"

"No changes in alkaline levels, respiration, heart rate, or body odor," Theremin reported. "She's telling the truth."

"I told you!" Tootie pumped her fist.

"Sorry, Tootie," Shelly said.

"You should know me better than that by now, Shell," Tootie said.

"Still friends?" Shelly asked meekly.

Tootie nodded. "Yup. Especially if you let me finish my pancakes in peace."

"No problem!" Shelly said, and she, Newton, and Theremin took their places in the food line. A few minutes later they were seated at their usual table. Shelly was sipping a Super Smoothie, as Newton squeezed wiggly green glop from a large tube onto his plate, then just stared down at it.

"Not interested in your kelp gel?" Shelly said.

"I'm just not hungry," Newton said as he pushed his plate away. "I'm still bummed out about my glitchy portal pass."

"I feel you," Theremin said. "I'm bummed out *all* the time because, one: I won't ever be able to see snow, and two: I'm me. But for you, you don't have any memories and are trying to find out about yourself and your family. That must be even worse than me being me."

"It is," Newton said. Then he thought of something that cheered him up a little bit. "Theremin, I have a feeling that you might get to see snow someday. Don't lose hope."

Theremin sighed. "I wish you were right."

"EMERGENCY!" someone yelled.

Suddenly, a giant hologram of Mumtaz's head and upper body appeared near the cafeteria's serving section.

"Students, I'm declaring an emergency!" she boomed. "There are reports that a dangerous monster is somewhere loose in Franken-Sci High. These reports must be taken very seriously. If you see this creature, do not try to engage it. Back away slowly, exit the area, and report it to me immediately. Fortunately, Stubbins Crouch has been working on a new Monster Neutralizer device, and this is the perfect time to test it."

Mumtaz's hologram flickered and was replaced by the image of what resembled a sinister-looking golf cart outfitted with a laser cannon, several mechanical claws, and multiple buttons and levers.

"With quick action this threat to Franken-Sci High will be captured before the fourth period bell."

Then Mumtaz's face reappeared. She smiled. "Have a great day!"

The hologram collapsed into itself as Shelly gasped.

"That wasn't a monster-catching machine!" she cried. "That was a monster-destroying machine!"

"It did look pretty serious," Newton agreed.

"We've got to stop Crouch from using it!" Shelly said.

"For all we know, this so-called 'dangerous' monster might be completely harmless. After all, it hasn't hurt anybody."

"Not yet," Theremin said.

"Maybe not *ever*!" Shelly said, shaking her head. "Honestly, I like Headmistress Mumtaz, but she's overreacting. If I were in charge, I wouldn't be sending out Crouch and his . . . his monster killing machine! I'd try to find a humane way to trap the poor creature and help it find somewhere safe to live."

"Why don't you, then?" Theremin challenged her.

Shelly's eyes brightened. "You're right, Theremin! I'll make my own cruelty-free monster trap! And you guys can help me!" she cried. Then she jumped up from the table and ran off.

Newton looked at Theremin. "Think we should follow her?"

"We'd better," Theremin replied. "When Shelly decides to do something, she doesn't stop until it's done!"

CHAPTER 9

Monster Trap!

As the rest of the campus was on high alert, Newton and Theremin spent the weekend in the Franken-Sci High Engineering Lab with Shelly as she worked feverishly on her humane monster trap. For hours she sketched different designs, mumbling to herself, and occasionally tossing out questions.

"Theremin, can you do some calculations for me? Newton, think these air holes are large enough?"

She refused to leave the lab, and the boys had to bring her food from the cafeteria or else she wouldn't eat. Newton studied her the whole time, fascinated. He knew Shelly was so passionate about her project because she cared so much about helping the monster.

Before I lost my memory, I wonder if I ever cared about anything as much as Shelly cares about her monsters and animals, he thought.

Newton brushed the question away and picked up

his tablet. Dozens of emergency announcements filled the screen.

"There was another monster sighting this morning," Newton read aloud. "In the gym."

"And Crouch . . . ?" Shelly asked, alarmed.

Newton shook his head. "No luck. He hasn't found a thing."

Shelly sighed with relief. "Good. Then we've still got time!"

The next morning, Shelly was ready to build her trap, and Newton and Theremin had a lot more to do. Theremin used his eye lasers to cut the metal pieces, and Newton helped Shelly fuse them together.

While they were working, Mimi dropped by the lab.

"I see what you're doing," she said. "Building some *thingamabob* to spy on me!"

Shelly turned off her molecular welding torch and rolled her eyes. "No, Mimi. We're building a humane trap for the monster that's on the loose. I'm going to save it before Crouch hurts it with his Monster Neutralizer."

Mimi's eyes narrowed. "Well, la-dee-da, and if it works, wouldn't you be the hero of the school?" she asked. Newton could tell from the sound of Mimi's voice that she was jealous. She stepped closer to Shelly's trap. "It looks too complicated to work."

"Actually, it's a fairly simple design," Shelly said, motioning to the large metal box they were constructing. "There will be bait inside, and when the monster steps in to investigate, it will trigger a door to slam shut behind it."

Shelly demonstrated by pressing on the floor inside the trap and then quickly pulling away before the door came sliding down. "See? I just need to sew together a big beanbag cushion so the monster is comfortable after it gets caught, and install soft lighting to keep it calm."

"We also need to figure out the bait," Newton said.

"Yeah," Shelly added, "every monster I've ever known has a sweet tooth, so the bait could be candy or something like that."

Mimi nodded. "Looks okay."

"Thanks, I think." Shelly smiled.

"Even though it's amateurish," Mimi sniffed. "I'd better be going," she said. "I've got more *important* things to do."

As she exited, Mimi looked back over her shoulder and said, "Toodle-oo, Newton."

"Good-bye," Newton replied.

As Mimi disappeared out the door, Theremin

mumbled, "She didn't say good-bye to me."

"She doesn't have a crush on you, Theremin," Shelly said as she looked at Newton.

Newton blushed. "Mimi does not have a crush on me."

"Come on, Newton, she asked you out on a date," Shelly teased. "And you're the only one in this school who she's even *remotely* nice to."

"If she wants to be nice to me, what's wrong with that?" Newton asked with a shrug.

"Nothing, but I didn't like the look on her face when she left," Theremin said. "I think she's up to something."

"And Mimi is *always* up to something," Shelly pointed out. "Okay, who wants to get me some gummy cockroaches from the vending machine upstairs? I think they'll make great bait."

They worked into the night, until Shelly could barely keep her eyes open.

"Come on," Newton said, nudging her awake. "Let's get some sleep. We can finish tomorrow after school."

Shelly nodded, yawning. "Okay. I just hope the monster is safe until then!"

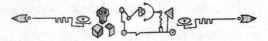

Monday morning, Newton, Shelly, and Theremin were walking to the school building when they saw an enormous crate being wheeled inside by two workers in green uniforms.

"What is that?" Newton wondered.

Just then, Mimi raced up. "Oh good! It's here!" she announced.

"What's here?" Theremin asked.

Mimi turned to them with a smug grin on her face. "It's *my* monster-catching machine, that's what!" she said. "The top scientists at my family's company have been working on it since yesterday, and they shipped it here this morning through the portal."

Shelly's eyes narrowed. "What? What do you want with a monster-catching machine?" she asked.

"The same as you, of course," Mimi said innocently. "There's a poor, innocent *monster-wonster* out there wandering around the school grounds all alone. I just want to capture it safely. And if, by chance, I get all the glory and some kind of amazing award from the school and one of the buildings named after me, well, that's just a bonus."

"Funny you didn't mention this yesterday." Shelly glared.

"Can we see your machine?" Newton asked.

"Absolutely!" Mimi said as she batted her eyelashes. Then she turned to the workers. "Open it up now!"

The workers quickly pried open the crate, revealing Mimi's monster-catching machine.

It was a clear plastic cube that looked a lot like Shelly's machine. Coiled springs extended from the sides, each with a shiny ball on the end.

"The shiny balls will attract the monster's attention," Mimi explained. "When it gets close, it will smell the bait inside."

She pointed to round green pellets inside the trap. "My scientists formulated the perfect organic monster bait candy, based on all available data of monster dietary habits," she said. "When the monster steps inside the trap, it triggers the door, trapping it inside."

Shelly put her hands on her hips. "You stole my design!"

"*Improved* on your design, not stole," Mimi replied, grinning. She pointed to a small metal device pinned to the side of her top. "And *this* will sound as soon as my monster . . . I mean, the school's monster is trapped! Your trap can't do that, can it, Shelly?"

Shelly frowned. "Well no, but—"

"Of course, you're welcome to set up *your* trap if you want," Mimi interrupted her. "Then we'll see whose trap is better."

Shelly grabbed Newton by the arm.

"Come on," she said. "We're getting my machine!"

"What about class?" Newton asked.

"Not important," Shelly answered.

"What about breakfast?" Theremin asked.

"Less important," Shelly said. "I'm not gonna let Mimi catch this monster first. No way."

Shelly, Newton, and Theremin raced back to the engineering lab. They put the finishing touches on Shelly's monster trap. Then Theremin used his super robot strength to carry it up to the gym.

"This is where the monster was last spotted," Shelly explained as they walked. "So, it's a good place to put the—"

She stopped short. Mimi had already set up her machine at the gym entrance.

"I guess you two had the same idea," Newton said.

"Uh-huh. Again," Shelly said. "Come on, let's try another spot. The monster might be hiding out in the basement. Let's put my trap there."

By the time they got the machine set up, they had missed their morning classes, and it was time for lunch. When they got to the cafeteria, they saw Mimi surrounded by a crowd of frightened students as she described her monster trap.

"The school will be safe any minute now," Mimi was

saying. "No monster will be able to resist my trap!"

"That's what *she* thinks," Shelly muttered.

Newton's stomach was rumbling. "Can we get some food now?"

"I'll meet you at our table," Theremin said, and he floated off.

Shelly and Newton got on the lunch line. Newton read the menu. "Pineapple pizza," he said. "What does that do? Boost brain power? Give you extra energy?"

Shelly shook her head. "None of those things. It's just the most diabolical thing you can do to pizza, adding pineapple to it. Only a mad scientist could have invented it."

They got their pizza and met Theremin at the lunch table. Newton settled in and took a bite.

"Isn't it awful?" Shelly asked.

Newton shrugged. "No, I like it . . . maybe because I'm so hungry!"

Shelly glared at Mimi. "No, I mean *her*! All those kids think she's so great. And she stole my idea!"

"I've been thinking about that," Newton said. "She did steal your idea. But if she catches the monster safely, that's all that matters, right?"

Shelly frowned, then sighed. "You're right, Newton. If it helps save the monster from Crouch, I'll be happy."

As they bit into their pizza, an alarm sounded from

the other side of the cafeteria. Then they heard Mimi shriek.

"I did it! I caught the monster!" she cried. Arms waving over her head, she ran out of the cafeteria, followed by everyone at her table.

Newton, Shelly, and Theremin looked at one another and then took off after the others.

When they got to the gym, a crowd of kids had gathered around Mimi's monster trap—and they were all laughing.

"Let me through!" Mimi said, pushing her way through the crowd. "I caught the monster, it's MINE! I want to see it!"

The crowd parted, and Mimi gasped.

Inside the monster trap, Professor Snollygoster was snoring loudly, sound asleep on a pile of comfy pillows. His mouth was stained green from the half-eaten green pellets in his hand.

Mimi started banging on the cube. "Professor, wake up! Get out of there!"

Newton looked over at Shelly, who was smiling for the first time all day.

"Looks like you made the perfect trap, Mimi," Shelly said. "The perfect trap for catching a tired professor with a sweet tooth!"

Mimi glared at Shelly, turned back to the trap, and kept pounding against the plastic. "Professor! You're trespassing!"

"See?" Newton said as she gently jabbed Shelly. "I bet you're going to catch the monster after all."

"I hope so," Shelly said. "Let's go check on it."

Then the class bell rang.

"I know I'm not usually the voice of reason," Theremin piped up. "But maybe we shouldn't miss any more classes today? No telling what Father will do if he finds out."

Shelly nodded. "You're right. We can check the trap after school."

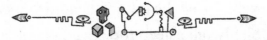

They all met in the basement after classes. The trap door was still open and the pile of gummy roach bait was still there.

"We can come back and check later," Theremin suggested.

Shelly shook her head. "I'm gonna stay here," she said. She pointed down the dim hallway. "I'm going to set up a secret observation post. If the monster appears from any direction, I'll see it."

"Then, we'll wait with you," Newton offered.

"Thanks but no. I'll be okay." Shelly said.

"After everything you've done for me?" Newton said as he motioned to Theremin. "For us? We're inseparable, we need each other, we're a team."

"Besides," Theremin added, "we don't have anything better to do,"

"Okay," Shelly smiled. "Thanks!"

They rigged up a hidden observation post with some big pieces of cardboard and discarded motherboards from the recycling pile. They sat on upside-down plastic buckets. Newton got snacks from the vending machine.

Then they waited. And waited. And waited. But the mysterious monster didn't appear. After a few hours Newton's eyelids grew heavy, his head drooped, and he fell asleep. Shelly fell asleep too.

"It's a good thing that I don't need to sleep," Theremin boasted loudly, but his two friends didn't stir. "Then again, I haven't recharged my batteries lately, so—"

Fffwaaaaaaap!

A loud electronic sound echoed through the basement. Shelly and Newton bolted awake.

"The trap!" Shelly cried. "Theremin, did you see anything?"

Theremin shook his head. "I was too busy watching you guys sleep."

126

They crept out from their hiding place and slowly tiptoed toward Shelly's trap. It shook, and a strange muffled sound came from inside the box.

"Something's in there!" Shelly whispered excitedly.

"I hope it's not another professor," Theremin mumbled.

Shelly took a deep breath, stopped, and looked at Newton and Theremin. "Stand back!"

She opened the door to the trap and jumped aside.

"Oh, uh, hi guys!"

Higgy, without his usual clothes, oozed out of the monster trap.

"Higgy?" Newton asked.

"Hi, roomie," Higgy said. "What are you doing here?"

"No, no. What are *you* doing here?" Newton asked.

"I was out on my nightly search for food when I came across a fresh batch of gummy cockroaches," Higgy said. "They seemed to be free for the taking, but when I went to scoop them up, I became trapped in this contraption. I was about to try to ooze my way out."

"There isn't a monster in there, is there?" Theremin asked.

"Nope," Higgy said. "Just what's left of the sugary . . . *burp* . . . you know."

Shelly sighed. "I guess I'm no more of a monster trapper than Mimi is," she said sadly. She turned and started to walk away. "Good night, guys. Maybe tomorrow we'll have better luck."

"I'll walk with you, Shelly!" Theremin said as he floated after her.

Newton turned to Higgy. "We'll take the tunnels back to our room," Newton said.

"Yes, that's fine, I am quite satisfied with my nightly snack," Higgy said to Newton as they made their way through the dark basement. "You haven't been around much these days, roomie. Is our plan still on for tomorrow?"

Newton had almost forgotten about their big plan. "Yes, sure . . . the plan! Everything's ready. I can distract him, if you can set him up."

"I can't wait," Higgy replied as the two roommates crawled into a nearby vent and made their way back up to their dorm room.

CHAPTER 10

It's a Rooftop Showdown!

The next day, Shelly kept running to the basement to check her monster trap between classes. Every time she returned, she looked disappointed.

"Nothing yet," she would report.

When the last class bell rang, Shelly ran to check on her monster trap.

Newton turned to Theremin. "We should go help Shelly."

"Actually, I was going to go back to my room," Theremin said. "Last night I upgraded to a level seven warrior in *Ultra-Mech Apocalyptic Showdown.*"

Newton's eyes widened. "You're a student, a robot, AND a soldier?"

"Dude, it's a computer game," Theremin answered. "I guess you don't remember anything about those either, huh?"

Newton shook his head.

"Then I'll show you!" Theremin said, starting to zip away.

"Wait! Let's first check in with Shelly," Newton said. "After all, if she did trap the monster, she'll need our help."

"Okay, if we can make it fast," Theremin relented.

When they got to the basement, they found Shelly sitting inside the observation post.

"Still nothing," she said. "But I have a feeling it will happen soon."

"I didn't hear about any more monster sightings, did you?" Newton asked.

Shelly shook her head. "Nope. I bet the poor thing's scared and hiding out."

"Well, it looks like you've got this under control," Theremin said. "Later."

As he started to zoom away, Newton called after him. "Room for one more in that soldier game?"

"Sure," Theremin asked. "I can teach you how to play. You'll have to start at level zero, though. You'll lose lives a lot at first, but I'll talk you through it."

"It sounds dangerous," Newton said.

"It's not real, Newton. It's all on the computer," Theremin said. "It's not dangerous at all."

They stepped outside, into the rain forest. Newton stopped.

"You know, Theremin, there's a lot I don't know about this island," Newton said. "Like this thing here. What is it?"

"It's a coconut palm," Theremin replied.

"And what about that thing there?" Newton asked, pointing to a multi-colored bird with purple-gold plumage.

"That's a bird—a crimson topaz," Theremin said. "Can we do this lesson on island flora and fauna some other time? I can get to level eight before midnight if I start playing right now."

"Oh sure," Newton said. He started walking again, but really slowly.

"Newton, is something wrong with you?" Theremin asked. "You're acting weird."

"That's the story of my life. Acting weird, right?" Newton asked.

Theremin shrugged. They entered the boys' dorm and walked up the stairs to Theremin's room. Newton stood back as Theremin opened the door.

"I'll set up the screen for two players and—what?"

Theremin stopped short. Inside his dorm room, snow was falling from the ceiling! Piles of it already covered the floor.

"Is this . . ." Theremin's voice trailed off.

"It's real snow, Theremin," Newton said. "Since your dad won't let you off the island to see it, Higgy and I brought some to you."

Higgy's face popped out from behind the door. He handed Theremin a knit cap, mittens, and a scarf to help keep his metal exterior safe and dry.

"I got an *A* on my weather-machine projector last semester," Higgy said as Theremin bundled up.

"This is . . . awesome!" Theremin cried, floating around the room.

Higgy reached down with a gloved hand and scooped up some snow. "I covered all your stuff with plastic before I turned on the machine," he said.

Theremin smiled. "I've gotta text Shelly about this!" he said as he extended his arm and began typing on a keyboard built into his wrist.

Newton stepped inside the room and stared up at the falling snow. "It's beautiful," he said. "And I guess this is my first time seeing snow too. At least, the first that I remember."

"I've always wanted to build a snowman," Theremin said.

"I think we should definitely do that!" Newton agreed. "But first, put on Higgy's coat so you don't get snow on you."

The inside of Higgy's coat was covered in green goo, so Theremin said, "No thanks. I'll just be sure to dry off when we're done so I don't get rusty."

They were shaping the bottom of the snowman when Shelly walked in.

"Theremin, what's so—oh!" she exclaimed. "Snow!"

"It's a gift from Newton and Higgy," Theremin said. "Since Father won't let me use my portal pass."

"This is awesome!" Shelly said, smiling. "Can I help with the snowman?"

"Sure," Theremin replied, but before Shelly could take a step, a scream came from the hallway.

Everyone turned to see dozens of students running down the hall and screaming, "Monster! Monster!"

Newton and his friends quickly helped Theremin wipe snow off his metal body. Then they followed the others, who all ran downstairs and outside to the lawn.

A crowd of students had gathered and were pointing to the top of the building. Newton looked up.

"Whoa!" Newton cried.

A truly terrible creature was snarling and snorting on top of the dorm roof. It had deep blue fur, four legs, six arms, three eyes, and sharp spikes running along the top of its head.

Then it dropped its jaw and with an earth-shattering

"Abbblrdrrrrpp!" it shot fire from its mouth.

The crowd screamed and backed up.

The only student who didn't move was Shelly. She had a shocked look on her face. It was the shock of recognition. "I know that noise," she said. "It's Peewee!"

"That thing's not peewee at all," Theremin said. "It's as big as a house!"

"No, its name is Peewee," Shelly said. "At least, I think it is. It looks kind of like a monster I found last summer in Transylvania. It followed me to our hotel and wouldn't leave my side, so I took it home and named it Peewee. But when I started school, it was small, smaller than a kitten."

"Abbblrdrrrrpp!"

The enormous creature spewed more fire, forcing everyone to step back even farther.

"Somebody get Mr. Crouch!" a student yelled.

"No!" Shelly cried. "I'll save you, Peewee!"

She ran into the building. Newton and Theremin looked at each other—and then ran after their friend.

Shelly was fast. By the time Newton and Theremin got to the roof, she was already slowly advancing toward the monster.

"Peewee, is that you? It's me, Shelly!"

The monster turned and focused its eyes on Shelly.

"Abbblrdrrrrpp?"

"Careful, Shelly!" Newton cried.

The monster didn't shoot fire this time. It reached out to Shelly, and then it wrapped one of its arms around her waist. She didn't flinch.

"That's it, Peewee," Shelly said soothingly. "I won't hurt you."

The monster then lifted Shelly high over its head.

"Hey, put her down, you big . . . BULLY!" Theremin yelled.

The monster's head snapped around and it fixed it eyes on Theremin.

"Abbblrdrrrrpp!"

Newton and Theremin jumped out of the way just as the stream of fire shot past them.

"No, Peewee! Bad Peewee!" Shelly scolded.

Then Newton heard pounding feet behind him and turned to see Headmistress Mumtaz and Custodian Crouch emerge from the staircase onto the rooftop. Crouch was steering his Monster-Neutralizer machine and aimed the fearsome-looking laser cannon at the monster.

"Don't do it!" Shelly cried. "Peewee's not hurting me! He's very affectionate!"

"This monster is a danger to everyone at the school,"

Crouch said. "Jump down, Shelly!"

"I won't!" Shelly replied. "I can't, anyway, because Peewee won't let go!"

"I'll try not to hit you, then," Crouch said. He pressed a button on his machine, and it began to hum loudly as the laser chamber powered up.

"Mr. Crouch," Mumtaz leaned closer, "have you tested this thing?"

"Of course not," Crouch replied as he squinted and directed the laser at Peewee. "I didn't have a dangerous monster to test it with until now."

"Shut it down, then!" she said. "You'll hurt Shelly!"

"Abbblrdrrrrpp!"

The monster shot a stream of fire at Crouch that fell just short of hitting him. Angry at the close call, Crouch continued aiming the Monster Neutralizer at Peewee.

"Noooooooooooo!" Shelly cried, waving her arms frantically.

Instinct kicked in, and Newton leaped at Crouch, knocking him off his machine and onto the rooftop. The Monster Neutralizer fired, sending a powerful beam of pulsing energy harmlessly into the sky.

An instant later . . . *Poof!* Professor Flubitus appeared on the roof, behind Peewee.

The absentminded professor was looking around,

checking in his pockets. "Oh dear. I seem to have misplaced my . . ." He reached up to his face. "Oh, here it is!" he muttered. Then he pulled a toothpick-size device from where it was resting in the hair above his ear. He aimed the device . . . a rainbow beam shot out and hit the monster. Peewee's eyes rolled back and he slumped to the ground.

"Noooo! What have you done?" Shelly screamed.

CHAPTER 11

The Heartsick Monster

"Don't worry, I just zapped the beast with a somniosleep inducer." Dr. Flubitus smiled. "But it won't last for long. We need to get it somewhere safe before it starts attacking people again."

Mumtaz spoke into her wristwatch. "Get the detention room ready. We've got our mystery monster coming down." Then the headmistress looked at Flubitus. "Would you please teleport the monster there, professor?"

Flubitus didn't reply. He had begun muttering to himself again.

"Flubitus!" Mumtaz yelled.

He raised his hand but still wasn't paying attention. "Present! I mean . . . do you mean, me?"

"Well, you're the only one on this roof named Flubitus, and the only one with a pocket teleporter," Mumtaz said, momentarily getting impatient with him.

"Obviously, that's how you got here. Can you please beam the monster down to the detention room?"

"Without hesitation," Flubitus replied. He grabbed hold of the sleeping monster's fur with one hand, pulled the mini-teleporter from his pocket, and pressed the button.

Streams of crackling electricity burst from the device, ran up the professor's arm, and then expanded to surround him and Peewee and, *poof!* Flubitus and the monster dematerialized.

Shelly turned to run for the stairs, but Mumtaz grabbed her by the shoulder. "Not so fast, Shelly. We're going to my office. I need to know everything *you* know about this monster."

Shelly nodded. "Yes, ma'am."

Crouch grunted as he got to his feet, then frowned at his broken Monster Neutralizer. "I could have stopped the monster, Headmistress," he said. "The wind must have knocked me over."

This caught Newton's attention. *What a weird thing to say*, he thought, since *he* was the one who had knocked Crouch off his machine.

Shelly spoke up quickly. "Yes, of course, it must have been the *wind!*"

"Hmm, that is odd," Mumtaz said as she held her

hand up in the air to check for a breeze. "There's no wind up here at all now."

"Well, uh . . ." Shelly was thinking quickly. "That's the wind for you. It comes and goes." She turned and smiled at Ms. Mumtaz. "Can I meet you in your office in a few minutes? I dropped my phone when Peewee picked me up, and I need to find it."

"I'll give you exactly one minute," Mumtaz said sternly as she and Crouch left the roof.

Shelly scoured the rooftop and said in an excited whisper, "They're gone, Newton. You can show yourself now."

"What are you talking about?" Newton asked.

Shelly turned in the direction of his voice. "Oh, there you are!" she said, looking down at the rooftop. "I can see the bar code on your foot. But the rest of you is camouflaged."

"Camouflage?" Newton asked.

"You blend into your environment when you're afraid, remember?"

Newton looked down at himself. Shelly was right. He saw the bar code on his foot, but the rest of him looked like the rooftop.

"Um, how do I become visible again?" he asked.

"It's already started," Shelly told him. "I think you go

back to normal once you feel safe."

"Whoa!" Theremin said in awe as Newton slowly materialized beside Shelly. "I sure wish *I* could do that!"

Newton held his hands up. They had returned to normal.

"I didn't even realize I was doing that!" he remarked. "Good thing that Crouch couldn't see me when I knocked him down. I would be in big trouble right now."

"It's weird, though," Theremin remarked. "Didn't they notice that you suddenly disappeared?"

"It was so crazy up here," Shelly replied, "they probably just thought that Newton ran away. Anyway, my minute's up. Gotta see Mumtaz. I was just lying about my phone so I could find you, Newton. And I really need permission to go see Peewee!"

Newton and Theremin walked with Shelly to the headmistress's office.

"Well, you three are like three peas in a pod, aren't you?" Mumtaz remarked when they came in.

"We're . . . ," Newton said, confused, "green and edible?"

"No, it means you stick together," Mumtaz said patiently. "Now then, take a seat. Shelly, please tell me what you know about this mystery monster. Where did it come from? And more importantly, who created it?"

"Well, last summer my parents and I were at our annual Ravenholt family reunion in Transylvania," Shelly said slowly. "I got bored and was walking through the woods when this teeny-tiny monster peeked out from behind a rock. I was really excited when it came right up to me and started making that cute *'Abbblrdrrrrpp'* noise!"

Newton and Theremin blinked then in unison. "You mean that tiny monster was . . . ?"

Shelly nodded. "Yes, I think it was Peewee. Anyway, I took measurements, pictures, and made my field notes. Then I left the little guy in its natural environment, like any good monster naturalist would do."

"I wouldn't expect anything less, Shelly," Ms. Mumtaz said. "So, what happened?"

"Well," Shelly said with a sigh, "Peewee followed me all the way back to our hotel. And he wouldn't leave my side. He had bonded with me. I figured he had lost his family somehow, and he needed me."

"And you took him home," Mumtaz deduced.

Shelly nodded. "But I have no idea how he got *here*!"

Mumtaz frowned thoughtfully. "Okay, so if this is Peewee, and he's been looking for you all this time . . . I thought you said he was small?"

"Yeah, really small," Shelly replied. "And he only had two arms and two eyes and he didn't breathe fire . . ."

Suddenly, the room rumbled as they heard a distant cry. "*Abbblrdrrrrpp.*"

"Are you sure it's the monster downstairs?" the headmistress asked.

Shelly sighed. "Well, he kinda looks like Peewee. And he makes the same sound. Maybe he's just grown-up? And you saw what happened on the roof. He picked me up gently. He didn't hurt me. I think he wanted to protect me."

"I believe you, Shelly," Theremin said. "Besides, it's kind of weird that the monster just showed up here. Isn't it logical that it was looking for Shelly?"

Newton was still confused. "But how did it get here?" he asked. "I thought the only way to get onto Franken-Sci High Island and off again is by using a portal."

"That's absolutely, one hundred percent true," Ms. Mumtaz said, "for humans."

"*And* robots," Theremin added.

"I beg your pardon, Theremin," Mumtaz smiled. "But for monsters, no matter what size and shape, the Bermuda Triangle is a very strong attractor for them. Peewee must have found a way in, especially if he was tracking Shelly."

Newton thought about this. *Strange that Peewee had found his way to Franken-Sci High at the exact same time as . . .*

"Dr. Flubitus!" Newton yelled. "Ms. Mumtaz, the new professor must have brought Peewee here!" he said. "They both showed up around the same time. Besides, there's something really, really weird about Flubitus. He's been following me all over campus!"

"Oh dear." Mumtaz sighed. "Flubitus means well, but he can be very clumsy. I can assure you, he didn't bring the monster to this school."

"But how do you know that?" Newton asked. "And what about him sneaking around following me?"

"Professor Flubitus is harmless, trust me, Newton," Mumtaz said. "He is looking out for the best interests of you . . . and Shelly."

Shelly looked surprised. "You mean he is following me, too?"

"Hey!" Theremin said as he pushed his way between Newton and Shelly. "Why not me?"

The headmistress looked at the robot kindly. "You don't play a role in this situation right now, Theremin. But you *can* still help your friends."

"Help us with what?" Newton asked.

"And what situation?" Shelly added.

Mumtaz stood up. "All I can tell you is that there is nothing to worry about," she said. "Dr. Flubitus is completely harmless. Now, Shelly, I'm sure you are anxious to see your monster. Professor Leviathan is examining him at the pool, and then we'll probably keep Peewee there so he can swim."

Newton's head began to fill with more and more questions, but the headmistress clearly had ended the discussion.

"We'll go with you, Shelly," Newton said, and the

three friends left the headmistress's office.

"This is getting really weird," Theremin said out in the hallway. "Flubitus is following you two on purpose? And Mumtaz knew about it?"

"Definitely weird," Shelly agreed. "And something we need to investigate. But first, I have to see Peewee."

They made their way up to the indoor swimming pool where a transparent hard-shell containment bubble had been placed over the whole thing. Peewee was inside, nervously pacing back and forth on the floor on the side of the pool. Professor Leviathan stood outside the bubble taking notes on her electronic tablet. Beside her was Tootie.

"What are you doing here?" Shelly asked.

"I was with Professor Leviathan when she got the message to examine the monster," Tootie explained. "I just had to see it for myself. Isn't it deliciously monstrous?"

Suddenly, Peewee saw Shelly. The monster charged up to the side of the bubble and crashed into it.

"*Abbblrdrrrrpp!*" it wailed. Fire shot from its mouth, but it fizzled harmlessly against the bubble.

"Uh, Shelly," Professor Leviathan observed. "This creature seems to know you."

Shelly nodded. "Yeah, I'm sure it's Peewee," she said,

and then she launched into the story of how she found the monster at her family reunion.

"Found it!" Leviathan said as she held up her tablet. "The best match for Peewee seems to be a Transylvanian baccatrei. Except this one is much, much bigger. And has four extra arms and an extra eye. And spikes on his head. And breathes fire."

The tablet had an illustration of the baccatrei in its usual tiny form.

"That's exactly what Peewee looked like when I found him," Shelly said.

Peewee began pounding his arms against the containment bubble. "*Abbblrdrrrrpp!!!*"

Shelly continued, "But obviously he's changed. Maybe this happens when they grow up."

Leviathan shook her head. "Not according to this documentation. They're supposed to stay the same size and shape."

Tootie's eyes widened. "Wait! In class we turned a butterfly into a giant monster with a nanochip. What if Peewee got ahold of a nanochip too?"

Shelly slapped her forehead. "Of course! That's it! But how did it—" Then she frowned as she leaned into Tootie. "Did *you* do this? Did you transmutate Peewee?"

"No!" Tootie yelled. "I had nothing to do with this

monster. Don't you believe me?"

"I don't know. Only a member of the Monster Club would know about the nanochips," Shelly shot back.

Theremin interrupted. "I believe her, Shelly," he said. "Why would she even *suggest* the nanochip if secretly she's the one who used it?"

"Don't bother, Theremin," Tootie said. "Shelly's never gonna believe me."

Then she stomped off.

Newton turned to Professor Leviathan. "If there's a nanochip inside Peewee, can't you deactivate it?"

"It depends on how the chip was programmed," the professor replied. "First, let's determine if there really is a nanochip somewhere inside our friend here. I keep them locked up and catalogued in my lab."

Shelly smiled weakly as she approached the bubble and pressed her hand against it. Inside, the monster pressed one of his hands against hers as, one by one, Peewee's giant eyes filled with tears.

"We have to figure this out," she said. "Poor Peewee!"

The group left the gym and went to Professor Leviathan's monster lab. The professor touched the wall. A panel slid open, revealing an old-fashioned banker's safe. Leviathan opened it by twirling a combination lock and removed a metal tray filled with glass vials.

She counted them, then frowned.

"Hmm," she said quietly, "strange."

Then she pressed a band on her wrist and activated a hologram catalog showing pictures of the vials to find the most recent one. Sure enough, there was an extra vial in the latest picture.

"One vial is missing," she reported.

"I knew it!" Shelly said.

Theremin floated over to the open safe. "Professor Leviathan, okay if I look for clues with my magni-vision opti-scope?"

"Go for it," the professor said.

White beams shot from Theremin's eyes as he scanned the open safe from top to bottom. Then he scanned the surrounding wall, the ceiling, and the floor.

"Aha!" Theremin cried. He pivoted forward and picked something off the floor. Then he held up his find between his metal fingers. "A monster tooth!"

Newton looked closer and gasped. Stuck to the tooth was a strand of bright green hair.

"Flubitus!"

Clues and Clones

"It was him!" Newton cried. "Flubitus stole the vial containing a nanochip and used it to turn Peewee into a monster."

Leviathan laughed nervously. "Not so fast, Newton, let's not jump to conclusions," she said. "Professor Flubitus is harmless, trust me."

"That's exactly what Ms. Mumtaz said," Newton told her. "But I don't believe it." Newton held up the strand of green hair. "This is proof that he stole the nanochip!"

"It's only proof that he was in my office," Leviathan said. "Now, why don't you three run along."

"But what about Peewee?" Shelly asked. She wanted to make sure Peewee was safe, and even though she trusted Ms. Mumtaz, she wasn't sure what some of the professors might do to him.

"I'll find a way to neutralize the nanochip," the professor replied. "Don't worry. Your monster will be fine until then."

Shelly started to argue, but Leviathan pushed them all out of the office and slammed the door behind her.

"This is so wrong!" Shelly cried. "If Flubitus is the one who turned sweet, innocent Peewee into a giant monster, we've got to find a way to prove it."

Newton nodded. "I've got an idea. Let's sneak into his office tonight and look for clues."

"But he's almost always following you," Theremin pointed out. "How can we do that without him knowing?"

"I have an idea about that, too," Newton said, and he explained it to Theremin and Shelly.

"Brilliant!" Shelly cried. "We'll meet in your room at eight oh-five on the dot."

"I'll tell Higgy the plan," Newton said.

"Good," Shelly said, then remembered something. "But first, I need to do something. Will you guys come with me?"

Five minutes later they were in the girls' dorm, knocking on Tootie's door.

"Who is it?" came a voice from inside.

"Shelly!" Shelly said.

"Go away!" Tootie replied.

"And Theremin and Newton!" Theremin added.

There was a pause.

"Come in!"

Shelly opened the door, and they stepped inside a room containing bunk beds and a wall lined with shelves filled with chrono-chess-ball trophies and monster action figures. Tootie was stretched out on the bottom bunk on her back, staring upward.

"Tootie, I owe you a big apology," Shelly said.

"You sure do," Tootie said.

"I was so worried about Peewee I wasn't thinking straight," Shelly explained. "He's more than a monster to me. He's my friend."

"That makes two of us, Shell," Tootie softened. "Some of my best friends are monsters too."

"That's why I know you'll forgive me. You're the only one in the school who loves monsters as much as I do."

Tootie nodded.

"Maybe I also felt a little bit like you were going to take my place, or make better monsters than me, or something," Shelly confessed. "I didn't realize it till now, but being related to the Frankensteins, I put a lot of pressure on myself to be the best at everything related to monsters. But now I want to put all that aside and just be friends, okay?"

Tootie sat up in her bunk and extended a hand to Shelly. "I get it," she said, pumping Shelly's hand. "Friends it is! That's what I wanted all along."

"Thank you, Tootie," said Shelly.

The two girls hugged for a moment, and then Theremin interrupted. He wanted to show off his new toy.

"Hey, Tootie! Friends are cool, but snow is even cooler. Want to build a snowman in my room?"

"Why not?" Tootie grinned. "I love snow."

As Theremin and Tootie left the room together, Theremin winked at Newton.

"See you later, pal," he said. "Eight oh-five on the dot."

"I'm going to check on Peewee again," Shelly said.

Newton nodded. "And I'm going to ask Higgy for a little favor."

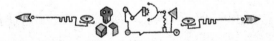

At eight p.m., it appeared that Newton left his dorm room and made his way down the hall, but it was actually Higgy dressed in Newton's clothes. As the disguised Higgy turned the corner, he noticed Professor Flubitus following some twenty feet behind him.

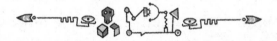

At exactly 8:05 p.m., Shelly and Theremin knocked on Newton's dorm door—and the *real* Newton let them in.

"How long do you think Higgy can keep Flubitus occupied?" Shelly asked.

"For as long as we need," Newton replied. "Before he put on my clothes, Higgy slurped down a bucket of chocolate pudding. So he's all fueled up."

Then Newton, Shelly, and Theremin wriggled under the bottom bunk bed and dropped through the secret trapdoor that led to the school's underground tunnels. Higgy used the tunnels to scrounge for food from the cafeteria at night because he was always hungry. But the dark, dank passageways were also useful for sneaking around campus without being noticed.

The three friends crept through the tunnels, not stopping until they stood beneath a specific vent. Newton easily jumped up and pushed open the vent, and then pulled himself up into Professor Flubitus's classroom. Newton pulled Shelly up, then Theremin used his rocket boosters to shoot up through the vent.

"So, what are we looking for again?" Theremin asked.

"Anything that proves that nasty old Flubitus is here to cause trouble," Shelly replied.

"Yeah," Newton agreed. "Look at everything that's connected to the guy. He appeared on campus at the same time as Peewee *and* we know he stole the nanochip that turned Peewee into a monster!"

"Poor little Peewee." Shelly sighed.

"Plus, he's been following me," Newton continued, "and Shelly too, according to Headmistress Mumtaz."

"What a mess," Shelly said as she looked through a pile of papers on the professor's desk. "Here's a formula for growing ears on an orange, and a diagram for building battery-powered socks."

Newton and Theremin joined her.

"And a crossword puzzle," Theremin said as he held it up. "Hmm, what's a ten-letter word that means *dubious*?"

"I don't know, but none of this is very exciting," Newton sighed. "Just more papers with a bunch of numbers and this one with bar codes on it."

Shelly perked up. "Bar codes?" She grabbed the sheet from Newton.

"Is that important?" Newton asked.

"Maybe," Shelly said as she touched the side of her glasses and took a picture of it. "Theremin can scan these bar codes when we have more time."

They searched through Flubitus's desk drawers next, and while they found a rubber chicken, a multi-dimensional odor detector, and a bag of freeze-dried smog, nothing proved that Flubitus was anything but odd and probably harmless.

"Nothing suspicious here at all," Newton grunted.

"Hey, that's it! A ten-letter word for *dubious* is *suspicious*!"

"Thanks, Newton!" Theremin said as he scribbled the answer on the crossword puzzle.

"Come on, there's nothing here," Shelly said.

A few minutes later they were back in Newton and Higgy's room. Shelly sat on the floor and retrieved the photo she had taken. With the press of a button, her lens filled with the sheet of bar codes.

"What's the big deal about bar codes?" Newton asked. "We saw them the first day that Flubitus taught class."

"Well, it might be a big deal," Shelly said, "because you have one on your foot, Newton, and Mumtaz *did* confirm that Flubitus is following you!"

Newton removed his sneakers and socks and picked up his left foot to show the black bar code stamp.

"Well, yeah, but it doesn't mean anything," Newton said. "Theremin can't even scan it."

"True, but it's not normal to have one," Theremin said.

"And remember when you went into camouflage mode on the roof? You totally blended in *except* for your bar code," Shelly said. "It *must* be special, somehow."

Newton shrugged. "Maybe, but to help figure out what this has to do with Flubitus, how about we make a list of what we know about Flubitus so far?"

"Sure," Shelly said, and she took her tablet and stylus out of her backpack and began to write. Her notes were projected into the air in front of them:

WHAT WE KNOW ABOUT PROFESSOR FLUBITUS:

HE ARRIVED DAYS BEFORE PEEWEE APPEARED ON CAMPUS.

HE'S BEEN FOLLOWING NEWTON.

A STRAND OF HIS GREEN HAIR WAS FOUND ON A TOOTH.

THE TOOTH WAS FOUND ON THE FLOOR IN THE ROOM WHERE LEVIATHAN KEEPS HER NANOCHIPS.

PROFESSOR LEVIATHAN SAID HE WAS HARMLESS.

HEADMISTRESS MUMTAZ ALSO SAID HE WAS HARMLESS.

MUMTAZ SAID HE IS "LOOKING OUT FOR THE BEST INTERESTS" OF NEWTON AND SHELLY.

"And Flubitus wants to buy a cloning device from Mimi's family," Theremin added.

"Thanks, Theremin," Shelly said. "I totally forgot that!" She added it to the list.

"I've scanned my memory banks twice now," the robot said. "And that's all we know about Flubitus. Unless the rubber chicken is important."

"You never know." Shelly shrugged. She added two more lines to the list.

HE WANTED TO BUY A CLONING MACHINE FROM MIMI'S FAMILY.

HE KEEPS A RUBBER CHICKEN IN HIS DESK.

Then she tapped her stylus against her chin thoughtfully. "Cloning . . . cloning . . ."

"Guys, what are bar codes used for, anyway?" Newton asked.

"They're placed on items for sale," Shelly explained. "When you scan the black lines, they give you information about the item. How much it costs, the product number, where it was made."

"So why do I have one?" Newton asked. "I'm not for sale."

"True," Theremin agreed. "But bar codes are also used to differentiate one thing from another, right? So maybe . . ." The gears were turning inside Theremin's head. "Just maybe your bar code is there . . ."

". . . so that someone can keep track of you!" Shelly completed.

Newton blinked. "But other humans don't have bar codes, right? I mean, you don't need bar codes to tell humans apart?"

"Nope," Theremin said. "You humans usually can be

163

differentiated by the way you look, your fingerprints, your DNA, and more." Then Theremin stopped and chuckled. "I guess you'd only need a bar code if there were, like, a bunch of other Newtons."

Shelly jumped up. "Theremin! That's it! A bunch of other Newtons!" She pointed to the list. "That's what clones are! Genetically identical animals or people. You *could* use a bar code to tell them apart."

"Are you saying *I'm* a clone?" Newton gulped. "That's too weird. Higgy pretending to be me is one thing, but I don't like the idea of a bunch of other Newtons running around."

"You're right," Shelly admitted. "It's too weird. Maybe the bar code is there so you can confirm your identity when you camouflage. Like, if you got stuck in camouflage mode or something."

Newton frowned, thinking. He didn't know much about himself. And he liked the idea that he was special. But if he were a clone, well, what did that mean about where he came from? Were there five, or fifty, or even a thousand other Newtons that looked just like him out in the universe?

Then Higgy burst into the dorm room.

"Oh good, you guys are back," he panted. "Flubitus is a good tracker. I led him all over the campus. He almost caught up to me, but he tripped over his feet a couple of times. I finally lost him when I turned to come back here and he went into the gym."

"The gym?" Shelly gasped. "That's where Peewee is!"

Without another word, she ran out of the room.

CHAPTER 13

Truth and Consequences

Newton, Theremin, and Higgy hurried after Shelly. They caught up to her halfway to the gym.

When they entered the pool area, they saw Flubitus stepping toward Peewee, who was still inside the containment bubble.

"Peewee!" Shelly yelled. The monster's eyes immediately turned and locked on her.

Dr. Flubitus raised his arm toward Peewee. There was something in the professor's hand! A prickly feeling of danger coursed through Newton. He charged up to the bubble.

"Flubitus! Get away from Shelly's pet!" Newton yelled.

"Dear boy, it's not what you think!" Flubitus called back, keeping his eyes on Peewee. "Well, at least I don't think it is. I'm afraid I don't know how to read minds quite yet. Wouldn't that be wonderful? Or would it be awful? It's hard to say. Now, if I could just get this thing to work!"

Newton spotted the door to the containment bubble and ran toward it. Peewee turned as Newton burst through the door.

"*Abbblrdrrrrpp!*"

A ribbon of flames streamed toward Newton. He sprang up, adhering to the top of the bubble with his grippy hands and feet.

Dr. Flubitus zapped Peewee with something.

Poof! Peewee shrank to the size of a mouse. He still had blue fur, but now only two legs, two arms, two eyes, and little bumps on top of his head instead of spikes.

"Peewee, you're back to normal!" Shelly cried, running in to the bubble.

"*Abbblrdrrrrpp!*" Peewee squeaked as he hopped up into Shelly's open arms and began to purr.

Newton dropped down from the top of the bubble. He landed in front of Dr. Flubitus and saw that he had a remote in his hand.

"You deactivated the nanochip!" Newton said.

Dr. Flubitus nodded. "Yes," he said. "Sorry it took me so long to make the correct calculations."

Theremin and Higgy entered the bubble.

"Aha!" Theremin said, pointing a metallic finger at Flubitus. "You *did* steal the nanochip! And you programmed it to turn Peewee into a monster!"

"Yes," he said. "But I never meant to harm the little one. Let's go to my classroom, and I'll explain."

Newton eyed him suspiciously. "No thanks."

"Anything you have to say to us," Shelly added, "you can say right here."

Dr. Flubitus sighed. "As you wish."

"And you've got a lot to explain," Newton said. "Why have you been following Shelly and me?"

"Why did you put the nanochip in Peewee?" Shelly asked.

"What do you need a cloning device for?" Newton said.

"And why is there a rubber chicken in your desk?" Theremin asked.

Flubitus nervously ran a hand through his green hair. "Let me begin with Newton's first question," Flubitus said as he looked at Newton and Shelly. "I was supposed to be watching over both of you, but you weren't always together so it wasn't possible. Then it occurred to me— if there were two of me, I could be in two places at once! Thus, my interest in the cloning machine. Without it, I just did the best I could by myself."

"But *why* were you following us?" Newton asked.

Dr. Flubitus ignored that question. "As for Peewee, when I arrived at the school, I found Peewee trying to get inside. I recognized him as the monster you found at your family reunion, Shelly."

Shelly gasped. "Have you been following me since last summer?"

Flubitus nodded. "Peewee didn't track you all the way to Franken-Sci High. I brought him in with me, to help him find you, Shelly. I couldn't reveal my real mission while I was trying to program the nanochip for Newton." Flubitus turned to face Newton. "To protect you."

Newton's head was spinning. "Wait, wait, what? You were gonna put the nanochip in me? You wanted me to grow extra legs, arms, and breathe fire?"

"Don't forget the spikes," Theremin added.

"Well, I hadn't quite perfected it yet. I was still working on the program when Peewee got a little hungry, and he ate the nanochip! When I started chasing him, the chip kicked in and he transformed into—well, you know the rest," he said, nodding to Shelly.

Shelly snuggled Peewee. "That's right. You were a big scary monster, weren't you, Peewee?"

"Abbblrdrrrrpp!"

"So, I had to work out how to neutralize the chip," Flubitus continued. "But all's well that ends well, I suppose."

"I don't think it's ended at all," Newton said. "Mumtaz, Leviathan—they both said we should trust you. But you were gonna turn me into a gigantic, fire-breathing monster!"

"Yes, well, with the benefit of hindsight, that doesn't seem wise," he said. "But you see, I really am just trying to protect you."

"Protect me from what?" Newton asked, his voice rising. "You're not answering my question!"

"He hasn't answered my question about the rubber chicken, either," Theremin mumbled.

"Oh dear me. It is tricky, you see," he said as he ran his hand through his hair. "I have to be very careful about what I tell you."

"Just tell us the truth," Newton said.

Dr. Flubitus took a deep breath. "Well you see, Newton . . . Shelly, I traveled a great distance to protect you," he said slowly. "A very long way."

"A long way from where?" Theremin asked.

"The future," Dr. Flubitus said.

"Whoa," Higgy burped.

Flubitus stepped closer to Newton and Shelly. He placed his hands on their shoulders.

"*Your* future," he finished. "And I'm afraid it's not looking so good."

Newton and Shelly turned and stared at each other for a very long time. . . .

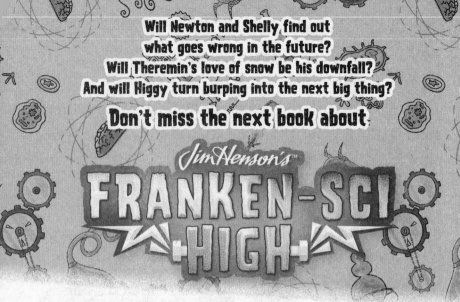

Will Newton and Shelly find out
what goes wrong in the future?
Will Theremin's love of snow be his downfall?
And will Higgy turn burping into the next big thing?
Don't miss the next book about

Jim Henson's™
FRANKEN-SCI
HIGH

THE ROBOT WHO KNEW TOO MUCH

When his robot friend Theremin Rozika aces a test that he was really nervous about, Newton Warp is surprised to see that his friend looks sad instead of happy. Theremin's father programmed him to never be smarter than his dear old dad: If Theremin begins to do well in one area of study, he immediately fails every other subject. So Newton and his friend Shelly Ravenholt attempt to reprogram Theremin, with disastrous results. Instead of making Theremin smarter, they accidentally make him speak in pig Latin! They're forced to contact Theremin's father, Dr. Rozika, to repair their friend's code. Can they also convince him to give Theremin the freedom to succeed?